#1 LALLY'S GAME

#1 LALLY'S GAME

BY

SCOTT CAWTHON
KELLY PARRA
ANDREA WAGGENER

Scholastic Inc.

Library of Congress Cataloging-in-Publication Data available

ISBN 978-1-338-82730-9

10 9 8 7 6 5 4 3 2 1   22 23 24 25 26

Printed in the U.S.A. 131

First printing 2022 • Book design by Jeff Shake

TABLE OF CONTENTS

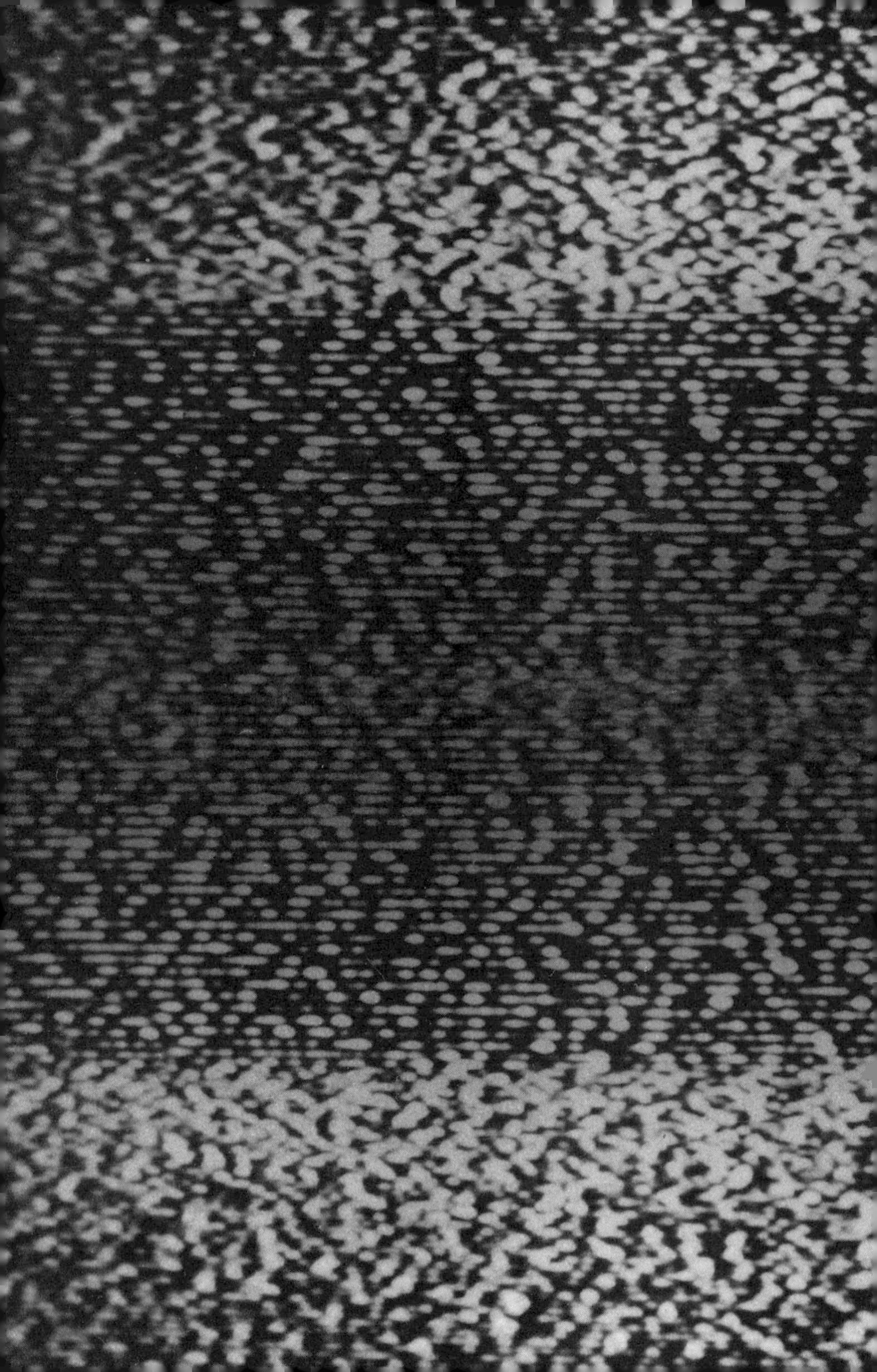

FRAILTY

THE NIGHT WAS COLD. RAINDROPS SCATTERED ACROSS THE ROAD LIKE TINY PELLETS. THE FLASH OF RED AND BLUE EMERGENCY LIGHTS REFLECTED OFF THE WET PAVEMENT AND THE WRECKAGE OF A CRASHED SEDAN AGAINST A BROKEN TREE.

"Come on, kid. Stay with me, stay with me," Jack, the EMT, whispered. Drops of rain rolled off his face while he pumped his hands against the rib cage of a teenaged boy.

"Clear!" his partner, Dave, yelled.

Jack raised his arms as Dave charged an electric current into the boy's heart. The boy's body jerked on the wet gravel road.

Jack started pumping the kid's chest again. "Come on, kid. Come back to us."

"Still no pulse, Jack. It's been too long. We got to call it."

"Once more. Come on, kid."

Again, they tried to revive the boy, but to no avail.

"Dang it." Jack sat back, wiped rain and sweat off his nose with his wrist. "Call it." After a moment of regret,

Jack covered the kid with a tarp. He stood up, gave himself a minute. It was always painful to lose someone so young.

He heard a rock skitter across the ground.

Jack swiveled his head toward the black brush from behind the tree. *Was someone there? Maybe an animal?* He couldn't see anything through the curtain of rain. He rolled his shoulders, picked up a medical bag, and turned away. "Let's pack up and get the coroner here."

"Kid didn't make it?" Officer Manor asked him on his way back to the ambulance.

Jack shook his head. "Not this time."

"Too bad. This road is dangerous, let alone during a storm like this."

"Don't I know it with the calls I've had here in the past . . ." Jack trailed off as he placed the bag into the van.

Officer Manor nudged his flashlight toward the dark. "And right here, near a cemetery of all places. Bad vibes, I think."

"Just a coincidence," Jack said.

A sudden movement caught his eye. Jack squinted against the rain and shifted his attention toward the body. There was a dark form in the rain. Was someone leaning over the corpse?

For a split second, the hairs on the back of his neck raised; then he shook the feeling off. He blinked to make sure his eyes weren't playing tricks on him.

There was someone. Short, slim, frail. The form hovered over the dead boy's body, doing some kind of motion with its hands, back and forth. Then he saw it.

A knife.

Jack stepped forward. "Hey! Get away from him!"

The dark form jumped up, long wet hair covering a face, light glistening off the weapon, and something swinging from the figure's hand. Then the little thing ran away back into the darkness of the brush.

"What happened, Jack?" Officer Manor asked, scanning the darkness.

Jack pointed toward the dark brush. "I saw someone. Leaning over the body. It—uh—it was a-another kid, I think. Maybe a girl."

Officer Manor walked around, shifting his flashlight around the scene. He came back with a slight twist on his lips. "You sure about that, Jack? A young kid walking around in this? How long's your shift been?"

Jack shrugged a shoulder. "Going on twenty-four. Yeah, I need some sleep."

"Maybe I shouldn't have mentioned the cemetery. Got you thinking of spooks in the night. I was only kidding around, you know."

Jack went back to the kid's body and picked up the last medical bag. Maybe he *was* imagining things.

The tarp moved.

Jack jumped. *"Holy heck, Dave—we got a live one!"*

"What?!"

"The kid! He moved! Get the gurney!"

"You sure?"

"Just get over here!"

Jack tore the tarp from the boy. He saw the kid's face smeared with blood, watched as the kid coughed, sucked in air.

The kid moaned. "H-help . . ."

Jack whipped out the portable oxygen and slipped the air mask over the boy's mouth. "It's okay, kid, breathe, we've got you. Nice and easy. You've been in an accident. We're taking you to the hospital, and they're going to take good care of you. Do you remember the accident?"

The boy gave a slight nod.

"Driving a little too fast in the rain. Wrapped around the tree pretty good. Hang in there, kid. You've just been gifted a miracle."

Jessica pushed the wet mop across the hospital floor. *To and fro. To and fro.* She remembered that saying from somewhere before . . . She just didn't remember from where.

Something from the past.

A shudder ran through her as her hands trembled on the stick of the mop. She tightened her grip so it would stop. She felt the hospital staff walk by her. She felt them look at her. She tilted her head forward so her thick, black hair curtained her face as much as possible. Not to be seen. Not to be noticed. No one said anything to her more than necessary. She did not speak to them unless spoken to. She performed her job each day after school and mopped the floors of the children's medical wing. She grew accustomed to the scent of sanitizing cleaner and the dismal odor of the sick. She listened to the murmurs of the staff. She paid attention to the beeps of medical machines hooked up to sick children. She studied the various footsteps she heard on the hard tiled floors. Sometimes soft steps, sometimes clicks of heels or stomps of bigger people. Sometimes the steps were rushed; sometimes they were slow. She was aware of each and every child in the hospital wing. She often heard crying and whispers of conversation as she cleaned the floors.

"The doctor says you're doing really well, Brian. You're eating better. Treatment is going well. That's wonderful, son," a woman's voice spoke from the patient's room that Jessica was near.

"Yeah, I guess so," Brian murmured.

"Hang in there, sport, You'll be better before you know it," a man said. "And then you'll get to come home and rest in your own bed."

"I have been feeling a little bit hungrier."

"That's so good to hear," the woman said.

"When will I get to go home?"

"I hope soon, son," the man said. "When you do, we'll get your favorite pizza from Freddy's Mega Pizzaplex. We'll make it a celebration. How does that sound?"

"Pretty good, actually," the boy said.

The man laughed. "That's my boy."

"Bri," spoke the woman. "What are all these strange flakes on your chest?"

"Huh?"

"Look, Harry. What are these? My gosh, what kind of hospital did we bring him to?"

"I don't know. They look like little bits of silver," the man said. "Relax, Jane, I'm sure there's a reasonable explanation. They've been taking good care of him here. You even said so yourself. He even looks better today."

"I know but . . ." The woman called out of the room, "Nurse Macy, please, can someone come to my son's room?"

"Yes, Mrs. Ramon. Is Brian okay?" Nurse Macy asked.

"Yes . . . but what is this strange stuff on my son? I don't want anything on him that is going to make him sicker."

"Hmm . . . I don't know what that is." The nurse went in and checked Brian's chest, and brushed the strange flakes off him. "I don't think it's anything serious, Mr. and Mrs. Ramon. I'll have staff sweep it up and get some new blankets."

"Please, I don't want any cleaner or anything on him that is going to harm his recovery."

"Yes, Mrs. Ramon. Don't worry, we would never let that happen."

Jessica pushed the mop slowly across the hallway.

To and fro. To and fro.

★ ★ ★

"She's so strange, that one," a nursing assistant murmured to Nurse Macy as they were stocking supplies on a medical cart.

"Hmm? Jessica, you mean? Quiet. Keeps to herself. Never makes any trouble." Nurse Macy shrugged. "Nothing wrong with that."

"Well, she's so frail. Looks like a feather could knock her over. Hair always covering her pretty face." He shuddered. "Creeps me out the way she lurks around. It's not normal. She's obviously alive, and yet she's not *really* living."

Nurse Macy shook her head. "You've been watching too many horror movies, Colin."

"How do you think people come up with these scary movie ideas? They see things that freak them out and write about them."

"I'm sure you were at an awkward stage at fourteen."

"We're not talking about me. Besides, I *talked* to people. I tried asking her something the other day and she just looked at me and blinked like I spoke an alien language or something."

Nurse Macy sighed. "Oh, Colin . . ."

Clang.

Just then, something dropped from behind them, making them jump.

Colin let out a childish *eeek.*

Nurse Macy glanced down to see a rusted tin can lying on the hospital floor.

She frowned. "That's odd. Where did that come

from?" she murmured. She glanced left and right, and spotted Jessica mopping not far from them.

"Oh, Jessica, would you mind picking up this can and throwing it away? I don't know where it came from. Must have dropped off a kitchen cart or something. I'll have to tell them to be more careful with their garbage."

Jessica gave a silent nod, and, dragging the mop, picked up the can, and threw it in a nearby trash can.

"Thank you. Oh, and, Jessica?"

Jessica slowly lifted her head, her hair parting to reveal her delicate features. Her eyes were dark. *Didn't they used to be a brighter brown?* wondered Nurse Macy.

One small beauty mark was dotted high on her left lovely cheek, but her skin seemed to have lost some of the rosy flush it once had. Her lips were delicate and full. Her face was slim and so pretty. She really could be featured in magazines.

"You're doing a good job for us." Nurse Macy gave her a small smile.

Jessica smiled, and it seemed to brighten her despondent features.

"I'm glad." Jessica spoke quietly, but the *glad* didn't reach her eyes.

"I bet you're a big help at home with your family. Do you help with cleaning around the house with your mom or dad?"

Nurse Macy watched Jessica merely nod and turn away to continue mopping down the hall.

"I'm telling you—creepy," Colin said under his breath.

Nurse Macy just waved her hand at him. "Oh, hush. She's just a young girl and you're a grown man. I think you could take her on if she attacked you."

Colin shuddered. "Don't be so sure."

Even though Nurse Macy joked with Colin, she could admit to herself, and not explain why, that peering into Jessica's dark gaze nearly broke her heart.

On her break, Jessica walked into the hospital chapel. The room was empty of grieving family members. She liked it that way, to have the chapel all to herself. It was rare, but it was peaceful and quiet and allowed her to pray. She ran her hand softly over the wooden pews that lined the walkway to the alter, and chose the first seat. At the front of the room was a large wooden cross hanging on the wall. She smelled the fresh white flowers set out for display on both sides of the room. There were three rows of small candles waiting to be lit. Quiet instrumental music played through a wall speaker.

She pulled the thick silver chain that hung around her neck from beneath her shirt and lifted it over her head, placing the pendant in her palm. The pendant had once been a whole heart, much larger and thicker. Now it was slightly bigger than a crescent moon, about the width of her thumb, with rough scratches embedded on one side.

Nearly finished.

She clasped her hands around the pendant and closed her eyes.

Please help me do good and continue with my purpose. Please help me make a difference. Please help me help others who are sick. Give me the strength to right my wrongs. Give me the courage to do what's right.

Thank you—

"Hello, miss, are you doing okay?"

Jessica blinked and stopped praying. She hadn't heard anyone enter the chapel. She looked over to see the priest standing beside the pew. He wore a black suit with a white collar. His hair was dark with streaks of gray, and his eyebrows were thick over kind brown eyes. There were tiny lines beside his eyes when he smiled.

"I'm fine," she responded quietly.

"My name is Father Jeremiah. I've seen you here before. What's your name, miss?"

"Jessica." Jessica cast her gaze down and rubbed her thumb across the pendant.

"Is there anything I can help you with, Jessica?"

Jessica shook her head. "No, thank you."

Father Jeremiah took a seat on the pew across from hers. "You look pale, Jessica. Are you feeling okay? Is there something I can get for you? A snack? Some water? Should you be resting?"

"I feel fine. I think . . . I probably look better when I'm working."

"Working?"

"Here at the hospital, in the children's wing. I help keep the floors clean." *To and fro. To and fro.* "Nurse Macy says I'm doing a good job," she added.

She hoped she was doing a good job. This job had been the perfect opportunity to get closer to those who needed her help. It was rare for her to come across others who were sick in the outside world. She'd heard the car accident last night by chance. A miracle, some might call it. She'd heard the terrible screech of tires, the harsh crash of the car against the tree. It had taken her time to get there through the heavy rain. She had watched the ambulance come and the EMTs try to save the boy. They hadn't been able to save him. But she had.

She was glad she'd been there to help. She'd cut it close, though, and nearly been caught. She could never allow that to happen.

"Ah, yes, I know Nurse Macy. A very caring nurse." Father Jeremiah nodded. "I'm sure you're doing a good job." He cleared his throat. "You know, Jessica, some people come here asking for help in their prayers, and I often listen to those who have burdens to release or healing to experience. Expressing our worries, our problems, helps us to let go of what is heavy on our minds and hearts."

Jessica simply said, "That's nice."

She felt she was already letting go of something very important in her own way. She never shared her thoughts with anyone because no one would be able to truly understand what she was going through.

"If you ever feel the need to talk to someone, I am here nearly every day to speak with, should you choose. I'm happy to help in any way I can."

Jessica nodded her head, keeping her eyes downcast, as she rubbed the pendant with her thumb.

"What is that lovely charm you have there? It must be very special to you."

Jessica merely continued to rub her thumb over the pendant and didn't speak anymore.

After a moment, Father Jeremiah said softly, "Peace be with you, Jessica," and left her alone.

After a few more moments of prayer, Jessica slipped the chain back over her head and rose from the pew. As per her usual routine, she went to one of the single hospital restrooms. She locked the door and walked to the small mirror above the sink. She inspected the dark circles under her eyes and the paleness of her delicate skin. Some might think she was lovely, but the truth was she looked frailer each day. Being lovely was once all she had ever wanted. She could feel the weakness take over her body with each child she helped, with each scrape of the pendant.

She wore a black sweatshirt and black pants, and even black sneakers. Black wasn't a welcoming color. It kept people away from her. It helped her remember that she wasn't there to enjoy life but had to stay focused on her purpose.

From her pant pocket, she removed a compact powder. She opened the lid and patted the soft applicator to the powder and dotted her face with the concealer. It was a pretty soft ivory that gave her a fresher look. After she put the compact away, she pinched her cheekbones to give herself a little color. Her eyelashes were naturally dark and thick, and her lips full and pretty.

When she used to smile, people would smile back at her and be interested in what she said. Jessica used to feel that certain things were important, like how she looked, the best clothes, the coolest friends, the cutest boys, but they actually weren't as important as she had once thought.

Now everything was different, and she never smiled unless she had to.

Jessica left the bathroom to return to work. The lights were dimmed for the evening, and the staff had quieted down. As she pulled the mop and rolling pail from a cleaning closet, she heard the faint sound of cartoons playing nearby. Setting her mop aside, Jessica followed the sound to a new patient's room. A little boy with brown hair was curled up on his side, asleep, holding a green stuffed elephant. He was alone.

Jessica turned to glance behind her and saw no one looking in her direction. She walked quietly into the room and pulled her chain over her head, grasping the pendant. She slipped her knife out of her back pocket and opened the blade.

If someone walked in, they'd think she was trying to hurt him. No, she would never dream about hurting anyone. She wanted to help him in a way only she could. She never told anyone about her purpose of helping those who were sick. Others wouldn't be able to understand. She hadn't understood, either, until she received the shock of her life that she was no longer the girl she once had been.

Beside the bed of the little boy, Jessica began scraping roughly at the pendant with her pocket knife. Little shavings of silver drifted down on the boy as he slept. As she scraped, her chest seemed to tighten. Her pulse slowed and her breathing became shallow. These feelings in her body were how she knew she was helping this little boy heal.

When she felt it was enough, she slid the chain back over her head and the pendant once again under her shirt, closed the blade, and put the pocketknife away. The little boy blinked his eyes open. Blue eyes gazed at her with interest.

"Are you an angel?" he whispered.

"No," she whispered back, "I'm no angel. Go back to sleep."

"But I'm not sleepy."

Jessica's lips twitched. "Your eyes look pretty sleepy to me. I think if you close your eyes and count sheep, soon you'll get the rest you need to make yourself strong."

He scrunched up his nose. "Sheep? Why sheep?"

"Okay, what would you like to count, then?"

"I think I want to count . . . elephants. I like green elephants."

"Okay, you can count elephants. Go ahead—close your eyes and count."

The little boy closed his eyes as he said, "One green elephant, two green elephants, three . . ." Soon he drifted back to sleep.

Jessica turned to leave and nearly stumbled as a wave of weakness washed over her. Something skittered across the floor. She held on to the doorframe and balanced herself as the fainting feeling went away. She licked her dry lips and spotted a rusted spring just by the doorway. Her eyes widened. She quickly snatched up the spring and walked out of the room to finish her work for the evening.

Jessica sat alone at a lab table in Science and Engineering class at West Wilson High School. She preferred sitting alone, but it always seemed to happen naturally. No one dared to sit next to the weird girl who barely spoke, who barely participated in their world. She felt tired and distant. Mrs. Willoughby was droning on about a new project, and if she let herself, Jessica could drift off to another place in her mind, away from this present reality. She wasn't sure why she continued to go to school. Maybe it was to keep up the pretense. Her old life was now far behind her. There really was nothing here for her other than she didn't want to make things difficult by drawing attention to herself by missing school or even getting bad grades.

She really could do without the many scents of perfume, body odor, and junk food that surrounded her every day. The boring lectures, the teenage gossip, the stares from teachers and students. And not to mention the overall loudness of school—pounding feet, yelling voices, slamming lockers, music playing, cursing, crying, and laughing. So much *noise*. So many constant reminders of kids her age who were normal, with friends, teenage problems, and families at home who loved them even if they didn't always remember to be grateful for them.

Jessica had a home once. She'd had a family. She'd had everything and one day she gave it all up by making the wrong choice. If there was one thing Jessica had learned in her life, it was that some choices couldn't be reversed, and the only thing to do was move forward the best that she could.

"Look, it's the creepy girl," a student whispered behind her. Someone giggled.

"She barely speaks. What's the matter with her?" another girl wanted to know.

"She's like a mannequin who barely moves."

"Mark Johnson says she creeps around the graveyard."

"Oh my gosh—like a freaking zombie! Who would have thought West Wilson High would have its very own walking dead?"

Jessica didn't say a word. She'd heard it all before. *Zombie Girl. Mannequin. Dark Witch. The Walking Undead.* Although she did her best not to draw attention to herself, she still did. Just not the kind of attention she used to receive. She'd become the target of mean gossip, teasing, and sometimes pranks. Overall, she was a loner. A girl who was often avoided as she walked school hallways or sat in the cafeteria at lunch, which suited her just fine. The more she was avoided, the easier it was to check out of this present high school reality.

There were a few more whispers from the girls before something small hit the back of her head and dropped to the floor.

More laughs erupted. Even some laughs from the surrounding students.

Jessica smoothed her hair down with her hand, unbothered.

"Girls!" Mrs. Willoughby scolded. "Is there a problem?"

Mrs. Willoughby was on the younger side as a teacher. She wore dark-rimmed glasses and often sported a black ponytail. She was one of those teachers who spoke with her hands and was eager for class participation. She seemed to leave Jessica alone, though.

One of the girls cleared her throat. "No problem, Mrs. Willoughby."

"I would hope not. I think you girls would rather be out with your friends at lunch than helping me clean up the science lab today."

"No, we're good, Mrs. Willoughby."

"Thank you, you are so kind. Now may I continue without being *rudely* interrupted?"

"Yes, Mrs. Willoughby," the girls answered together.

At the lab table next to her, a boy picked up the used eraser that had bounced off Jessica's head. He tossed it back at the girls. "Real mature," he muttered.

"What's his problem?" the girl whispered, annoyed.

"He's new. He doesn't know the reality of Zombie Girl."

Jessica glanced at the boy and then looked away. He was indeed new to school.

"Okay, class, choose your partners," Mrs. Willoughby announced, with a clap of her hands. "Make sure to choose someone you know you can get work accomplished with instead of someone to goof around with until the last minute. This will be fifty percent of your quarter grade, so make it good."

Jessica blinked. *Choose your partners?* What had she missed?

The new boy stood and came to her table. "Hi," he said. "Want to be partners on the project?"

Jessica swallowed hard. She supposed she had to. It wasn't like she'd get another offer. She nodded.

He sat next to her in the empty chair. "I'm Robert."

"Jessica."

"This project is going to be kinda cool, huh?"

Jessica slowly nodded, unsure what it was about. She hadn't been paying attention. Robert had an athletic build, with honey hair, hazel eyes, and golden skin. He wore a pale blue collared T-shirt and faded jeans. There was a braided leather bracelet on his right wrist. He was the kind of boy from whom she would have wanted attention in her old life.

Now she wished she was invisible.

"I transferred from out of town," he continued. "My dad is an engineer and got a new job here. He was excited about this class for me." Robert brushed his hair back with his hand.

"Were *you* excited?" Jessica flinched. What was she doing? She was supposed to keep to herself.

"Yeah, it's fun, you know? Building stuff. But this will be my first time in a class like this."

Jessica nodded. She'd used to think building stuff was fun, too.

"Those girls were acting dumb," he said quietly, with a shrug of his shoulders. "There were girls like that at my other school. I never hung out with them. Just mean to everyone for no reason. They think it's cool, I guess, when . . . it's not."

"It doesn't bother me."

He lifted his eyebrows. "Really? That's cool. Most people wouldn't say that." Then he smiled. "I can't believe we get to build our own mini robot."

Jessica stared off in the distance. "Oh, perfect."

After school, Jessica was seated at a table in the school courtyard, waiting for Robert. They'd had a couple of class sessions to plan the bot project and decided to make a mini rolling bot that carried items on its back and was controlled with a remote. The catch was that they had to have the tray lift up and down. Robert had taken apart an old remote control car and discovered the components to make their bot active.

Robert dropped a cardboard box on the table, causing Jessica to recoil. He pulled out his old remote control car.

"I asked Mrs. Willoughby how much we can use from this on the bot. She gave me a list of what we can and can't use," Robert said, handing Jessica the paper. Today he wore a pale yellow shirt that buttoned down the front with gray sweats. Jessica wore her typical all-black outfit.

Jessica took the list he handed her. "We need to find other components for the ones we have to replace."

"Yeah, I know. What are you doing later? Mrs. Willoughby wants us to salvage as many components as we can instead of purchasing them. Maybe we can go to the junkyard and see what we can find."

Jessica quickly blinked a few times. "Um . . ."

"I know we need a couple of springs, something to be used as a tray. Maybe old wiring."

"I—I can't," she stumbled out.

"Huh?" Robert looked at her with a slight frown.

"I can't go there. I—I have to go to the hospital, to work. I forgot."

Robert shrugged. "Oh, well, we can go another day. We have time."

"*No*," Jessica said a little too sternly. She could feel her insides begin to shake. She started to pack her notebook into her bag. "I have to go."

Robert stared at her with surprise. "Now? I thought we were going to work on the project? We made a schedule. We should keep to it if we want to finish on time."

"Can't today. Tomorrow. You go to the junkyard, okay? It's not my thing."

"All right. It's for the project, you know. It's not like I like to hang out at junkyards, either. Uh, are you okay?" He grabbed Jessica's wrist, and Jessica pulled away as if stung. "Are you sick or something? You look a little pale."

"I don't feel well."

"Do you want me to walk you home? It's not a problem. I can come with you. Maybe you shouldn't be by yourself."

"No. I don't need help, okay? I'll see you tomorrow." She grabbed her bag and quickly rushed from the table. She felt faint, as if she could just keel over at any second. She managed to make it off school grounds and lean against a tree for support.

She grabbed her pendant with a shaky hand and closed her eyes. Her breath filtered out of her mouth quickly.

Everything is going to be okay.

Everything is going to be okay.

After a few moments, Jessica managed to calm her breathing. She licked her dry lips as she settled down. She didn't know what had come over her. She'd learned to steady her emotions or at least mask them from others. She couldn't let her emotions erupt like that again. It made her too vulnerable, and when she was vulnerable, she couldn't think straight. She set off toward the cemetery. The wind had picked up and was blowing her hair wildly. The cemetery had become her sanctuary in the recent months. A quiet, peaceful place.

When she stepped into the cemetery, she often stopped to read the headstones to get familiar with the souls who had been laid to rest. She wondered about her own grave and what her stone would read.

It was more than likely she would never get a burial.

As she strolled through the graves, her mind drifted back to Robert. She hadn't really met a boy so kind and confident before. If she let herself, she could start to *like* him—which was not possible now. Maybe in her old life she could have opened herself to having a true friendship, maybe something more.

But that all changed the day she made a choice.

And each day she was doing her best to make up for that choice.

She had a purpose now, and she was sticking to it.

She made her way to the farthest and oldest of family crypts. There hidden among the graves was a small mausoleum made of stone, with dark, stained-glass windows. Old, dried vines covered the top and hung down the sides of the structure, patched with white cobwebs. She gripped the rusted handle and leaned her foot on the bottom of the door, pushing with everything she had in her. The heavy door creaked open and scraped along the floor. Dust particles twirled in the sunlight. She pulled out her small flashlight and stepped inside, and pushed the door closed until she was surrounded by the dark. She switched on the flashlight and walked to the back of the small enclosure, passing what she assumed were a family of dead people named Holloway, then turned around a corner to a small sitting area that was made of stone. She'd cleared all the cobwebs of as many spiders as she could manage in this little hideaway. The groundskeeper neglected this section of the cemetery since the graves were over a century old.

She kneeled down on her sleeping bag and grabbed a pack of matches to light three yellow candles placed off to the side. She dropped her book bag and sat on the sleeping bag and pillow. Here she could let down her guard. No one could see her. No one could judge her. No one could wonder about her at all.

She was safe for now.

Next to her, she had a duffel bag of her signature black clothes. A small overnight kit with some makeup, a hairbrush, toothbrush, and toiletries. She kept her life simple. Minimal. She had one small item from her old life. She reached in the bag and took out a white rabbit's foot, and let it dangle from her finger on the short chain. She used to carry it with her everywhere, thinking it brought her good luck. Now she didn't believe in good luck. But it was a small reminder of who she used to be and who she would never be again.

She lay down on the sleeping bag and let herself rest before work.

Jessica noticed Nurse Macy was humming under her breath at the nurse's station while she was performing her mopping duties. It was mindless, really. Mindless in a weird kind of way. Weird was the theme of her life these days.

But what really concerned her was the fatigue that weighed down upon every inch of her body. Her grip on the mop was shaky, and even though she moved at a slow pace, she was tired. It was a bone-deep exhaustion that had been becoming more and more frequent each day. She used to have so much strength, and now she often wished for the time when the pendant had been a whole heart and she'd been full of energy.

The truth was, she'd been busy the last few nights with the patients.

She lifted a shaky hand to the pendant that lay under her shirt. It was definitely smaller now, thinner.

A tremor of fear vibrated down her spine. She lifted her chin. *She could do this*, she told herself. With as much strength as she could muster, she continued to push the mop.

To and fro. To and fro.

"Hi, Jessica, it's a lovely day, isn't it?" Nurse Macy mused, a wisp of a blonde curl shifting on her forehead as she walked over to her. Nurse Macy always wore scrubs in shades of orange, blue, green, or purple. Sometimes the patterns had funny characters or animal prints. Today there were cats making silly faces on her top. Her smile was welcoming, and even though Jessica did her best to keep her distance, Nurse Macy had this energy that pulled others toward her.

Jessica nodded.

"You want to know why it's a lovely day?" Nurse Macy asked.

Jessica paused and looked at her expectedly.

"Most of our patients in this wing have improved in some way!" she said, with a bright smile. "They are eating. Even smiling. Most times there's a heavy sadness that you feel around this floor. But now, today is a good day. When there are smiles and meals being eaten, and pain has decreased—it's like magic. In my line of work, you have to take the wins when you can get them, Jessica. You remember that."

Take the wins when you can get them.

Jessica liked that. She'd remember that advice.

Nurse Macy gazed into Jessica's eyes. "How are you feeling today, Jessica?"

Jessica looked away. "Good."

"That's nice. Anything new going on in your life? How's school?"

Jessica's grip tightened on the mop. "Nothing's new. Everything's good."

"Glad to hear it. Well, duty calls. See you later, gator."

Jessica watched her wave off to visit another patient. Even though she enjoyed being around Nurse Macy, it was getting harder to avoid her direct questions about her personal life.

She suddenly saw the nurse come to a halt right in the middle of the floor. "Sheesh, what is going on with all this junk? Jessica, there's an old fork on the floor. Would you mind cleaning it up? Between this and the weird flakes . . ."

Dang it. She missed another one. "Okay," Jessica answered.

Jessica slowly walked to the old fork and picked it up.

"A fork? Really?" she said quietly. Then she rolled her eyes and tossed it in the trash.

That was when she noticed someone new. There was a teenage girl about her age. She was lying in bed, wearing headphones. She had red hair and tiny freckles speckled across her cheeks. She solemnly played with the phone in her hand. There were three empty Jell-O cups on her side table.

Jessica pushed her mop pail closer to the room, and the girl noticed her.

She pulled off her headphones. "Hey," she said to Jessica.

"Hi," Jessica said.

"You work here?"

Jessica nodded.

The girl frowned. "Why would you want to spend your free time around sick kids?"

Because I want to help them.

"It's a job," she said instead.

"What's your name?" the girl asked.

"Jessica."

"I'm April. I was admitted early this morning. I'm not handling my treatment well this time around. You probably see a lot of kids like me around here."

"Sometimes," she said.

"Doesn't it bother you being around this?" She waved her arm around her.

Jessica shook her head. "Am I supposed to treat you differently?"

"No, but a lot of people do. You don't know how many times I see looks of pity or sadness and sometimes fear. Like if they are near me long enough, they might get sick, too. I don't see that in your eyes."

They stared at each other for a few moments. Then Jessica said, "Got to get back to work."

"Okay, um, you should stop by sometime. I'll be here, unfortunately. Eating lime Jell-O."

Jessica nodded as she pushed her pail away.

"I got some springs, wiring, some bolts, and metal slats. What do you think about this tray? It's an old one, but it's cool, right?" Robert said to Jessica as they sat at a lab table in class. "Just the right size for the mini bot."

Jessica sat quietly looking at the items Robert had apparently salvaged from the junkyard. She wanted to knock all the dirty junk off the table. But instead she sat still like a statue. Unmovable. Emotionless. As if the sight of the old garbage didn't bother her at all.

"You're not saying much," Robert said to her.

Jessica met his eyes, saw the curiosity, and looked away. "Yes, these will work fine."

"Great. After the other day, I thought maybe I'd done something wrong. Maybe you didn't want to be partners anymore." He shrugged. "It's kind of late to find new partners."

"No, I told you that I wasn't feeling well." She unclenched her fist and pointed to the tray. "This is just the right size. You did a good job."

"I know, right?" Robert pushed his hair back with his hand. "I got excited when I found it. This bot is going to be so cool, Jess. You just wait and see."

Jessica froze as she heard the old nickname that her closest friends had once called her. She felt a lump form in her throat, and she swallowed hard. She hadn't known how difficult it would be to interact more at school and with Robert on this project. It was taking so much willpower to keep her in her seat and not run from it all. Reminding her of the past and bringing more of it into the present was not what she wanted.

Mrs. Willoughby strolled by their table with her notebook to mark off their progress. "Nice, Robert and Jessica. You are both pulling together your components on time. I like your initiative." She looked over the blueprints they had put together. "Looks like your bot is coming together. Good job, you two. Let's see you start the build over the next few days and make some progress."

"Okay," Robert said with a smile.

Jessica nodded.

"How do you feel about the project, Jessica?" Mrs. Willoughby asked her directly.

Jessica balked. Mrs. Willoughby usually avoided

speaking with her. "Um, I feel good. It's going to be good," she replied awkwardly.

"How do you like working with Robert?"

Jessica glanced at Robert and then back to the pieces on the table. "Good," she mumbled. "He's a good partner."

"So is Jessica," Robert piped in. "She's worked really hard helping me with the design and keeping us on track."

"I'm glad we're *all good*, then," Mrs. Willoughby said, with a small smile. "I'll check back with you in a couple of days about your progress. Keep up the hard work."

Mrs. Willoughby walked to the next table and Jessica could feel her shoulders relax.

Robert rubbed his hands together, excitement lit in his eyes. "Let's get started, Jess."

Jessica watched Robert set out a few components for the structure of the mini bot. She was very aware that she hadn't yet moved to help. He'd set out four metal slats that they would connect for the framing of the mini bot. Three of the metal pieces were obviously old and from the junkyard. One piece looked fresh and newly purchased.

Go on, pick one up, she told herself. But she couldn't bring herself to move past her hesitation. The used parts were dirty and old, and stunk of rust and grease. They reminded her of things she'd rather forget. But she knew that she couldn't avoid this forever. She couldn't just have Robert do all the work on the mini bot. That wouldn't be fair.

Detachment was her greatest defense. Sometimes she

envisioned her feelings as if she was a possum. When a possum felt it was in danger or threatened, it froze into a catatonic state. Jessica imagined her feelings being just like that. When she was strong, she could manage to shut down her inner feelings until the threat was over. Right now, she was the possum.

Her aversion to this junk did not affect her.

In fact, she was very much frozen inside until the threat to her feelings had passed.

She slowly reached for the dirty metal slats. She felt the cold steel in her grip, and she brought it toward her. She stared at it as she turned it over and examined the rusted edges.

She could touch anything from the junkyard and be okay. It would not harm her or affect her feelings. She set it back down and rubbed her fingers against her pant leg and exhaled a deep breath.

Success.

Nurse Macy was checking on Billy's vitals. Color had come back to his cheeks, and his appetite had increased, which in turn gave him more energy.

"You're doing so well, Billy," she told him. "You're eating all your meals like a big boy and taking your medicine."

"I *am* a big boy!" he declared as he zoomed a toy airplane over her arm.

"Yes, you are."

"Hey, Nurse Macy, when will I get to see the angel again?"

"Angel?" Nurse Macy asked, with curiosity.

"Yeah, the angel who helped me feel better."

"Oh yeah? How did the angel make you feel better?"

"She came to me in the night, and then I felt better. I'm not sure how she did it. She must have used magic. I like her. I want to see her again."

"Wow, that's pretty cool. You must have a guardian angel looking over you, Billy."

Billy lifted his little fists up in triumph. "Yay, I have a guardian angel!"

As he shifted, tiny specks fluttered on his blanket.

Nurse Macy spotted the flakes of silver with dismay. What was this stuff? She quickly brushed them off Billy's blanket. "Yes, you are a lucky boy. I'll check on you later and bring you some pudding? How does that sound?"

"Yum! Chocolate, please."

"You got it," she said. "I'll be back in a bit."

Just then, there was a loud *clang* from outside Billy's room.

Nurse Macy started. "What in the world?"

She walked out of the room and in the center of the hallway she found—a piece of a car muffler? Frustration coursed through her. "This is getting ridiculous. Who is playing these pranks?" She spotted Jessica nearby, mopping. "Jessica, did you see someone drop this?"

Jessica's eyes widened. "Um, no, I didn't see anyone else in the hallway."

"Well, somebody thinks they are funny, and they're not," she said a little loud so the culprit would hear. "*So they'd better stop.* Please, Jessica, grab some gloves and throw this garbage out. I'm trying to keep a clean floor here. If I get a surprise visit from the higher-ups and they find this garbage around, we'll be in big trouble."

Jessica nodded and hurried to the janitor's closet.

Nurse Macy frowned. She'd called and checked with the nurses on the other floors, and no one else was seeing junk left around in their areas. It was just in the children's wing for some reason. She decided to take a walk around the floor to see if she could spot any more tricks happening around the patients' rooms. She turned down a corridor, and sure enough she found a couple of greasy bolts! *Disgusting.*

Nurse Macy gritted her teeth. Once she found out who was doing this, she was going to give them a good scolding on how dangerous it is to leave industrial objects on the floor for someone to trip over. Not to mention how unsanitary it was for her sick patients in the hospital. She might even turn them over to hospital security to give them a good scare. She slipped on the rubber gloves that were stuffed in her pocket and picked up the bolts and continued on until she found a small rusted can. She swiped that up, but she still didn't see anyone around. Then she found herself right in front of the hospital chapel.

Was the culprit inside? she wondered. She dumped the junk in a nearby trash bin along with the dirty gloves and stepped inside to peaceful music. There was an old woman sitting in the center of the pews, but Nurse Macy couldn't imagine that she was the prankster.

She stepped farther in and walked to the front of

the pews, looking around for anyone who might be suspicious.

"Hello," Father Jeremiah said from behind her.

Nurse Macy jumped and put a hand to her chest as she turned. "Hello, Father," she said quietly. "Sorry, didn't see you."

He lifted his thick eyebrows. "How are you today, Nurse Macy?"

"I am doing well, Father. How are you?"

"I am well. Coming in for a visit?"

She began to nod, and then her face heated from the fib. "Well, I'm looking for someone who has been playing some pranks around the children's floor. Leaving pieces of garbage around."

"Nothing serious, I hope."

"It could be, so I need to put a stop to it. But I can't seem to figure out who it is yet."

"I'm sure you'll discover your truth soon enough."

She nodded. "I hope so. Father, by the way, there's a young girl named April on our floor. It would be nice if you could visit her and put her in your prayers. She could use some cheering up."

"Thank you for telling me. I will do that. How is our friend Jessica doing?"

Nurse Macy smiled. "Oh, you know Jessica? She's doing okay, I think. She does a good job for us."

He frowned. "I worry about her. So frail. So quiet. I've been praying for her lately. She visits here often."

"That's nice, Father. I worry about her, too."

"She could use a friend, I think."

Nurse Macy nodded. "I think so."

Father Jeremiah smiled. "Well, peace be with you, Nurse Macy. Have a good rest of your day."

"Thanks, Father. Same to you."

"I hope you discover your prankster. Just remember to go easy on whoever it is. Everyone has a story that we don't yet know."

"Yes, Father. I'll remember that."

Nurse Macy sighed and started to return to work when her foot knocked against something. She bent down to pick it up.

She narrowed her eyes at the discovery. It was a rusty lock.

Jessica sat on a chair in Robert's dad's workshop as Robert soldered some wires into the mini bot. The workshop was pretty neat, she thought. Shelves with labeled boxes lined one wall. There was a worktable that sat against the opposite wall. And another worktable in the center that Robert was working on. She stood on the other side of the table wearing goggles. She had felt hesitant having this next meeting at his house. It was too close, too personal. But Jessica knew that they had to work together to get the mini bot completed, and the next step had to be soldering the mini bot's guts together and the arm that made the tray go up and down.

Robert turned off the soldering tool and lifted his goggles. "I think I've got it. You know, Jess, we really need to agree on a name for the mini bot."

She lifted her goggles to her forehead. "I like calling it Mini Bot."

Even though Jessica hadn't intended to be funny, Robert chuckled. "Mini Bot, the MB, huh?"

"Yes, we could just give it a number, like the Mini Bot 5000."

Robert made a face. "Not very original."

"Robots aren't always original. Sometimes they are just made from boring, old junkyard scraps." A heavy sadness suddenly came over Jessica, and she clenched her fists. She'd really thought she'd gotten over the sadness and pain of her predicament and had settled on overall acceptance. But lately, emotions and feelings had been coming back at the weirdest moments. Why now? What had changed?

"It's not always about where things started from, Jess. It's about what you make of all the pieces once you have them."

Jessica frowned.

"My dad told me that once, and it always stuck with me. Remember, he's an engineer. He's always creating something out of pieces."

"Knock, knock," said Robert's mom as she entered the workshop, holding a tray with a plate of brownies and two glasses of milk. "I thought you hardworking engineers could use some body fuel." She had honey-blonde hair just like Robert, but she was shorter and her face softer. Jessica noticed they had the same welcoming smile. His mom set the tray on the side worktable.

"Thanks, Mom," Robert said.

Jessica thought she should say something, too. "Yes, thank you."

"I hope you like brownies and milk, Jessica. Do you have any allergies?"

"No, I don't."

"Good, enjoy them," she said. "I look forward to seeing your finished mini robot."

Robert's mom left, and Robert grabbed the tray and brought it to their table. He set it down, grabbed a brownie, and took a bite. "These are the best," he said with a mouthful. "My mom is an awesome baker. Try one."

Jessica was hesitant to take one. She watched Robert chew his brownie, then gulp down some milk. The truth was, she used to love brownies. They were her favorite dessert. But she never treated herself anymore. Never allowed herself to enjoy sweets or anything that connected her to her old life. She believed she didn't deserve them anymore.

"Come on, you know you want one," Robert said to her.

Jessica tilted her head to the side. "I guess . . . I can have one."

"Are you not supposed to eat sugar or something?"

"Um, not really." Jessica reached for a brownie. She could already smell the cocoa and the butter. She took a small bite and closed her eyes. The brownie tasted heavenly!

"Oh my gosh. That's really good," she murmured, enjoying the sweet treat.

"I told you, the best. Baking is one of my mom's favorite hobbies. Um, you know, Jess," Robert said. "You haven't told me much about yourself or about your family. What do your parents do?"

Jessica blinked. "You never asked."

"Well—"

"And I'm not much into sharing," she interrupted in order to sidestep the conversation about family, and took another wonderful bite.

He smiled. "Like I couldn't tell. You're not like other girls."

"I know. I'm not trying to be conceited. I just know that I'm . . . different. Weird."

"I wouldn't call you weird. I mean, other girls I've met like to talk about themselves. Sometimes too much. Worry about a lot of drama. You handle things differently, quietly. It's nice."

Jessica didn't know what to say.

"Anyway," he continued on, then cleared his throat. "You know I'm new here and I don't have many friends."

"Yes."

"You heard about the prom coming up?"

She nodded. "I'm not a junior."

"I am."

Jessica met his eyes, and Robert seemed to blush. He brushed a nervous hand across his hair. "I wondered if you would like to go with me?"

"What?"

"To the prom. I thought it would be fun to go together."

Jessica stared at him in shock, her brownie half eaten in her hand. She was actually speechless. She'd worked so hard to separate herself from school, from others, to be as invisible as she could make herself, and now she'd met a new boy, who strangely didn't think she was weird and wanted to take her to the prom like a normal teenager.

"It's in a week," he said, quickly, to fill the silence. "Do you think you'll have to work? Maybe you can request it off."

"Um . . ."

His cheeks reddened. "I mean, if you want to go with me. Unless you were already asked—"

Who would ask Zombie Girl? "No one's asked me."

Robert smiled. "Then, what do you say, Jess? Would you like to go with me?"

That night, Jessica rushed to the hospital chapel. Her heart was beating fast. For the first time in a while, her goal was skewered, as if she couldn't see the finish line anymore.

And it didn't feel good at all.

She sat down on the first pew and stared off into space. She didn't know what to do. She had left Robert's awkwardly, telling him she had to find out if she could get the night off. She'd let him know.

And she'd come straight to the chapel for guidance.

She pulled the pendant over her head and clenched it in her hands, closing her eyes.

Please help me know what to do. Please guide me. I never thought this would happen. I had made a plan, and now things have changed. I did my best to keep to myself and do the right thing and now . . . everything seems to be falling apart.

"Should I pray with you, Jessica?" Father Jeremiah asked from beside her.

Jessica swallowed. "I don't know. I mean, if you want."

Father Jeremiah sat next to her. For a few moments, they sat in silence.

"I don't know what to do," Jessica finally spoke to Father Jeremiah as she stared down at her pendant. "I always believed this pendant gave me strength. So that when I worked around the sick children, I could give them a piece of it to help them, too. I had thought I had found this job for that reason. To help others. To redeem myself for the bad choice I'd made in the past. But now things are changing . . . and I find myself wondering if it's okay to give to myself again by having some of my own life back. Something normal. I'm not sure if it's okay, though. And the worst part is that I had been so certain that I was on the right path."

"Why do you feel you can't give to yourself, Jessica?"

"Because of the past." A tremor radiated through her body. *The past, the past. The horrible past.* "I—I just didn't make the right choice. I mean, that's how I got where I am. I gave up everything. So there had to be a good reason for that, right? And now I'm asking just for a little piece back. Not something so big, really. Just a little thing for myself. Is it too wrong to ask?"

Jessica looked down at her pendant. It was so slim now. Barely anything left. Was she too late to ask for something in return? Did she even deserve to ask? Why didn't she have an answer?

"Of course not. When we do work for others, we have to be open to receiving as well. If we over-give, we become out of balance and we can make ourselves ill or sad. Giving to others is a great gift, but yes, Jessica, giving back to ourselves is a gift as well. God loves all his children, and he wants everyone to feel happiness and love."

Jessica looked at him directly in the eyes for the first time. "Is that really true? How do you know?"

Father Jeremiah lifted his eyebrows. "Because I know it in my heart to be true."

Father Jeremiah watched Jessica slowly stand and leave, her head bent down in sadness. *Poor child*, he thought. He wished he could be of more help to her. But he knew from experience that he couldn't save everyone. He could only do his best to guide them. He began to rise when he looked down at the floor and found a metal circle with spikes on the edges. He picked it up, studying the object. Some kind of gear, it seemed. *That's odd*, he thought.

He frowned and glanced at the door Jessica had just exited.

Jessica walked back to the children's floor. The lights were lowered for the evening. She could hear the beeps of machines and oxygen blowing air. Most of the kids were asleep. However, April was still awake.

"Come in here, Jessica. I see you," April called to her.

Jessica had tried not to be noticed. She wasn't doing such a good job of that lately.

She stepped into April's room. "Hi."

"Where's your mop?" April wanted to know.

"Still in the cleaning closet."

There was a beat of silence between them.

"It's cancer in the blood, if you are wondering why I'm here," April told her. There were dark circles under her eyes like the ones Jessica had covered up with makeup. "I'll be losing my hair again soon. Bald will be the new me."

Jessica didn't respond.

"You're pretty," April said, studying her. "Tell me about your school. Your life. I've been in and out of school for the past couple of years. Missed out on a lot of stuff. My friends barely speak to me now. They don't know what to say. They think I don't want to hear how much fun they are having, but I do. I used to play basketball. I'm athletic. Or used to be. What I wouldn't give to run down a court and shoot baskets again . . . But now I can do that in my imagination. So you tell me. Please. Just for a few minutes, help me be part of your world."

Jessica grabbed her pendant hanging from her neck and rolled it back and forth on the chain. She knew she didn't really have a life. Not the one she really wanted. But if embellishing a little about how wonderful her life was would help April, then she would try to talk about herself.

Leaning against the wall, Jessica told her about Robert and the Mini Bot. She told her how nice and kind he was to her when others hadn't been. That the project was halfway complete and that he'd just asked her to the prom.

April listened with a smile and a few questions thrown in, with swoons over Robert and the possibility of going to the prom.

"Maybe one day, I'll get to go to the prom," April said. "I can dream, right?"

"You will go to the prom," Jessica said. "If you believe it."

"I can picture it. I would be completely healed. My hair would be full and healthy. I think I would have a bright pink dress or a green one, with matching shoes. I would go with a nice boy like your friend Robert. I would dance all night and laugh with friends. Maybe even be part of the royal prom court. Then we would all go out together somewhere, like the beach. We'd run around a small campfire and talk about our dreams. The stars and moon would shine down on us, and maybe the boy would give me his coat because I was cold. Then when it was quiet and we were alone, he would give me a kiss under the stars. It would be the best night of my life . . ."

Jessica pictured the scene along with April, but instead of April it was Jessica having the best night of her life at prom. Jessica felt herself yearn for a wonderful and normal experience just like April had described.

"I'm tired now." April lowered herself on the pillow and closed her eyes. "We'll talk again sometime, Jessica."

"Okay." Jessica clenched the pendant as she looked at April. *She could help April,* she thought. But was she supposed to help everyone? Father Jeremiah's words drifted into her head.

Giving to others is a great gift, but yes, Jessica, giving back to ourselves is a gift as well.

With guilt heavy on her shoulders, Jessica quietly drifted back into the dark hallway.

After school, Jessica and Robert were ready for a first test run with the mini bot. Robert wanted a quiet place so other students wouldn't bother them. Jessica suggested the cemetery. The day was sunny, and the cemetery was fairly empty of visitors.

"You were right. It is pretty quiet here," Robert said as he looked around.

"Yes, almost peaceful," Jessica said as she led him to a far empty section of a parking lot.

"How'd you end up finding this place?" he asked.

Jessica blinked. "Um, well . . ."

His eyes widened. "Oh, do you know someone buried here? Geez, I'm sorry."

"Oh, no. Never mind," she said, not having an explanation that he would understand. "Let's just get set up."

The small bot was melded together with various metal parts from the junkyard and the remaining components bought at the hardware store, with a flat tray on its back. The arm had been fused together with an aluminum tubing, with the wires tucked inside. It was not yet painted or officially named, but it was ready for a trial run.

Robert set the mini bot down and then placed a soda can on the back of its tray.

"Okay, Jess, this is our first test run for the Mini Bot 5000," Robert announced.

Jessica's eyes widened. "You named it after my choice? I thought you said it wasn't original enough?"

"Yeah, but it's the best name we have. And MB deserves one. So Mini Bot 5000 it is. You ready to take some notes?"

Lately, being with Robert and experiencing his kindness, Jessica felt an unfamiliar warmth inside her when she spent time with him and when he made nice gestures to her like choosing her name for the Mini Bot. She couldn't really remember feeling this way before. Or maybe it had been so long that she'd forgotten. She wasn't sure if that was wrong or right, but she knew she enjoyed *feeling* good.

She nodded. "Notebook, check."

"Okay, switching on the Mini Bot 5000. Turning on the remote. Here goes nothing." Robert pushed the knob on the controller forward. There was a pause, then the Mini Bot shifted an inch forward and started rolling!

"Yes, it's working!" Robert shouted.

Jessica smiled as excitement for creating something new rushed over her. "We actually did it!"

"Okay, here goes the ultimate test . . ." Robert pushed a button on the remote, and the tray rose slowly. Then he switched the button again, and the tray shifted back down.

"All right," he said with excitement. "The lift works!"

Robert directed the Mini Bot 5000 to turn right and then left, then back around to stop in front of Robert's feet right before a wheel surprisingly fell off. The Mini Bot 5000 fell to one side. The soda can tipped over and fell to the ground.

They stared at the wheel as it rolled off to the side. Then they laughed.

"We can fix that," he said, and smiled at Jessica. "We succeeded with our first run of the Mini Bot 5000. We make a good team, partner."

Jessica nodded. "Yes." She took a deep breath. "And, Robert?"

"Yeah?"

Something fluttered in her stomach. "I would like to go to the prom with you."

Robert's smile got bigger. "You would? *Awesome*," he said. "I'll get the tickets tomorrow at lunch. I can meet you at your house before the dance—"

"Um, no, I can meet you there. It'll be easier for me."

"Are you sure?"

"Yes."

"Oh, okay. We can go eat afterward if you want. I don't know all the good places to eat yet, but maybe you can tell me your favorite."

"Maybe."

"Just let me know what the color of your dress will be as soon as you know. So then I can try and match the tux if possible. Depends on what's available at the rental."

Color of the dress? "Oh, okay."

"All right, great, Jess. It'll be fun. You want to do the

honors and get this wheel back on Mini Bot 5000?" He offered her the socket wrench.

Jessica gave a small smile and took the wrench. "Sure."

Nurse Macy watched Jessica mopping the floor. Something was definitely off. Jessica stared into space, barely moving. Usually her head was down, as the girl was doing her best not to be noticed, and today it was like she was in a trance.

Nurse Macy recalled what Father Jeremiah had said.

She could use a friend, I think.

"Jessica, are you okay?" Nurse Macy asked her. "Do you need a break? How about some water? You could be dehydrated."

Jessica blinked. "No, I'm okay."

"Are you sure?"

Jessica nodded.

"If you need help with something, please don't hesitate to ask."

Jessica stared at her a moment, and Nurse Macy began to feel like Jessica would forget to speak when she finally blinked.

"I am going to the prom," she said.

Nurse Macy smiled, happily surprised. "That's wonderful! Who's the lucky boy?"

"His name is Robert. He's my science partner."

"I bet you're excited."

Jessica didn't answer.

"Is there something else bothering you?" Nurse Macy

asked her. She wished she knew what was going on in her mind.

"I've never been to the prom before. I don't know what to expect. And I don't know what to do about a dress."

Nurse Macy looked at Jessica with compassion. She wanted to ask her, what about her mom or dad? Or a sibling or a relative? But she felt those personal questions might shut down Jessica completely at this vulnerable moment. She didn't know Jessica's personal story, but she understood Jessica was fragile and secretive about her life. There appeared to be a sadness about her that never seemed to go away. In Nurse Macy's experience, deep trauma usually was the cause of that in the kids she cared for. Nurse Macy always had this drive within her to help others, especially caring for the young. Even though Jessica wasn't a patient, she could tell the girl needed her help.

"Do you need some assistance in that area?" she asked her softly.

Jessica stared down at the floor for a moment, then Nurse Macy watched her nod her head up and down. It was very hard for Jessica to ask for help, and Nurse Macy felt a glow in her chest that she trusted her enough to ask.

"I'm happy to help you, Jessica. I have an hour-long lunch break soon. We can go right to the department store and I'll give you some advice on a dress. How does that sound?"

"That would be . . . good."

"I'll grab you when it's time."

★ ★ ★

Jessica stood in a slim, ankle-length lilac dress in front of a mirror in the fitting area of a department store. There were pale flowers etched into the design. The material was soft on her skin and beneath her fingers as she brushed her hand down her hip. She couldn't recall feeling a dress so soft before. She'd tried on a few before this one. There had been so many colors of dresses—pink, white, blue, yellow, red, and black. Short dresses and long ones. Off the shoulder or with thin or thick straps. Puffy skirts or straight ones. Dresses that glittered or shined. She'd wanted to wear black, but Nurse Macy convinced her to try something with color. Jessica hadn't looked at the price tag, but she hardly used the money she got from the job at the hospital, so she had plenty of savings to buy the dress and some shoes.

"Jessica, you look stunning," Nurse Macy said, in her gleeful way.

Jessica really looked at herself. She'd lost more weight recently, but she was still pretty, with her high cheekbones and full lips. Her hair was still thick and shiny. Her shoulders and arms looked delicate in the dress. In the mirror, she saw her lips curve, and for just a moment, she could believe she was a regular girl buying a dress to go to the prom with a boy she liked and who liked her back. That her life was normal and perfect.

"I think I like it," she said with a small smile.

"I do, too. Let's get you some shoes to match."

Deep down, Jessica knew this was like a fairy tale, and everything could burst and go back to the way things were soon enough. She'd asked Father Jeremiah if this was okay, to allow herself to have something for herself, and *he* seemed to think it was okay. To her, Father Jeremiah represented life and death and forgiveness. He had to know what was right and what was wrong . . . right? Because now Jessica felt uncertain and fragile. Feelings she didn't feel comfortable with at all.

Nurse Macy brought over a matching pair of simple purple shoes. "What do you think?"

Jessica slipped them on, and her height went up two inches. "They fit."

"Not only do they fit, but they are perfect! You are going to look beautiful on prom night, Jessica, and you are going to have such a wonderful time. Can you walk okay?"

Jessica tried to walk and felt a little clumsy. "Oof. It's not as easy as it looks. I've seen lots of women wear heels . . . but they walk so naturally."

Nurse Macy giggled. "They were once like you. With some practice you'll get the hang of it in no time. Just know it's normal for your feet to feel a little sore, especially after dancing. Don't ask me why we wear these things and torture ourselves. But they make our feet look pretty, don't you think?"

"They do."

Jessica glanced at Nurse Macy in the mirror as she gave her tips on how to walk confidently. Nurse Macy had always been kind to her, just as she was kind to all her patients. When other people at the hospital avoided Jessica, Nurse Macy always tried to talk to her, and now she was here helping her when Jessica most needed it.

Once upon a time in her old life, Jessica may have considered her a true friend, and had she been a normal girl, she very much would have wanted to be a nurse just like Nurse Macy. Someone she admired for her positive attitude and the way she cared for her patients. Bringing joy to others who were ill truly was a gift just like the kind Father Jeremiah talked about.

"I bet your family will love the dress you've picked out," Nurse Macy said, searching Jessica's gaze in the mirror.

"Um," Jessica said as she tried to think of a response. She supposed a typical parent would have loved seeing their daughter in a pretty prom dress. But that wasn't the case for Jessica. She tried to think of something to say, but her mind went blank.

A saleslady walked by them in the fitting room and stopped. "Wow, your daughter looks gorgeous. Is this for prom?"

Jessica and Nurse Macy locked eyes in the mirror, and Jessica had no idea how to respond. She simply looked down at her shoes, her hair shielding her face.

"She does, doesn't she?" Nurse Macy suddenly said. "Yes, it is for prom and this is the perfect dress. We will definitely take the dress and the shoes!"

Jessica raised her head and blinked in astonishment. She didn't question why Nurse Macy didn't correct the saleslady about being her mom. She guessed it didn't really matter. Explanations took too much energy sometimes. It was better just to let others see what they wanted to see.

As Jessica continued to look at herself, she let hope spread inside her for the first time in a long time. Prom night was going to be perfect.

After her shift, Nurse Macy wanted a nice, hot meal while watching one of her favorite TV shows. She vowed she would get that soon enough. It had been about a week since she'd taken Jessica to buy her prom dress, and she'd been warring with herself about what she should do. Should she leave well enough alone and let Jessica's business be, or should she take action to help her?

She'd finally decided to take action.

Nurse Macy rechecked the copy of Jessica's work application that she'd submitted to the hospital and tried not to let the guilt get to her for invading the young girl's privacy—or violating HIPAA. She read Jessica's address and put it into her phone's GPS app to guide her to Jessica's home.

She felt she was doing this in Jessica's best interest by getting down to the truth of the teen's family life. Nurse Macy felt if she knew what was going on at home, then she would be able to help her. Maybe speak to her parents or her guardian. Explain her worries about Jessica's health and demeanor. Perhaps even let them know that Jessica needed some help emotionally.

Jessica was a wonderful girl. She deserved family support for things like prom. She deserved someone to care about her. She deserved to be happy.

Nurse Macy knew Jessica was hiding something about her home life, but she wasn't sure what it could be.

Yes, she had a habit of sticking her nose where it didn't belong, but that was what made her a darn good nurse. She investigated the facts to better help her patients, and with Jessica it was no different. When Nurse Macy saw someone in need, she reached out to help.

Especially when the poor girl had to ask her older coworker to help her get a dress for prom. Where was her mother or father? Or her guardian? Why wouldn't a fourteen-year-old have someone to turn to? It was so sad, and she just couldn't stand it.

A few minutes later, she drove down an older section of town. Some of the streetlights were burnt out and she could see many of the homes were run-down. There were a couple of boarded-up windows with graffiti sprayed across garage doors.

"Turn right on Cemetery Lane," her app relayed to her.

Nurse Macy turned right. The night was clear and the stars shined above the town. She drove past the cemetery and looking at the dark gravestones, felt a shiver crawl down her back. *The poor girl lives near the cemetery,* she realized. Down at the end of the road was the last dilapidated house on the block.

"Your destination is on your left."

Nurse Macy pulled along the sidewalk and parked her car. She got out and clicked her car fob to lock her doors. She took a deep breath and pulled her coat closer around her neck against the cold of the evening. She would simply explain to Jessica and her family that she was worried about her and wanted to make sure she was okay. Then she would ask to speak to her guardian alone and explain her worries. She didn't want to embarrass Jessica at all.

She walked up the cracked walkway to the door. The light was dim, and she could see the light on inside through the curtains. The paint was chipping off the house and door.

Nurse Macy knocked.

She heard a little dog bark and footsteps before the door swung open.

An old woman with glasses stood in the doorway. She had curlers in her hair and no teeth. Nurse Macy could tell by the way her lips were pursed. Her skin was wrinkled and pale. She wore an old, ripped robe the color of gray storm clouds.

"Yes?" the old woman said as she squinted at Nurse Macy through her thick glasses.

"Hello, my name is Nurse Macy—"

"Nurse? Don't need no checkup. Had one just the other day. Shush up, Pipsy," the old woman said to the little barking dog.

"Oh no, I work with Jessica. Are you her grandmother?" Nurse Macy could understand clearly why Jessica didn't have the support she needed. If she was living with her grandmother, she likely had to take care of this woman rather than the other way around.

"Who'd you say? Don't have my hearing aid in. Can't hear as good as I used to."

Nurse Macy leaned in closer. "*Jessica.* Is she here? May I speak with you about *Jessica*?"

"Jessi-ca? Don't know no Jessi-ca."

Nurse Macy blinked in confusion, she stepped back to look at the house number. "Um, is this 333 Cemetery Lane?"

"Yes, but you must have the wrong house. No Jessi-ca here. Now I need to get back to my shows. Don't want to buy nothing, either."

"Oh, well, I'm sorry. I don't know what happened—"

The door was shut in her face, and then the porch light turned off.

Nurse Macy sighed in frustration. "Where in the world are you, Jessica?"

Jessica was in total darkness. Her surroundings were completely quiet except for her breath. There was a coldness that penetrated her skin, straight to her bones, and she shivered. She touched her bare arms, and then her clothes. She felt the material of her prom dress. *Why am I wearing my prom dress?* she wondered. Where was she? She put her hands out in front of her, trying to feel her way forward, but she saw nothing in front of her and nothing behind her.

Fear crashed over her. She was nowhere.

Had she died in her sleep? Was this what the afterlife was like?

Was she in some kind of in-between world?

But she couldn't have died, she realized. It wasn't yet her time. She still had to go to the prom. She still had to help April. She felt for the pendant and gripped the metal that always felt warm to the touch. It was still around her neck.

She started to walk forward, with slow, hesitant steps. She didn't know how long she walked. It seemed like forever.

Out of nowhere, she finally heard a creak. A footstep? A movement?

"Hello," she whispered. "Is someone there? Please, if you are there, say something. I'm afraid. I can't see anything. *Please.* I don't know what to do."

No answer.

She licked her dry lips as she continued to move forward trying to get somewhere. Anywhere. Was there a wall? A door, maybe?

Another sound came from around her. Metal creaking against metal.

Jessica froze as awareness dawned. *No.*

The sound happened again, but this time right behind her.

A shudder of terror radiated down her spine.

Jessica ran.

She rushed forward as fast as she could, with her arms waving around her, wondering if she would collide with something.

Metal footsteps stomped behind her. Quickly, too quickly.

So close. So close.

She blinked, trying to adjust to the dark, but she still could not see anything.

In the cold, a sweat broke out on her body as she ran, trying to escape the terrifying thing that chased her.

A tense grip curled around her arm.

Jessica screamed. "No, please! Get away from me! Someone help me!"

Quickly, the grip tore off her arm from her shoulder.

She felt the warm gush of blood rush down the side of her body. Her body vibrated in shock. Her mouth opened, gasping for air.

Then she felt a grip on her other arm.

Jessica tried to yank away when she felt her arm pulled from her bone.

Jessica fell down in pain and agony, and it seemed like it took forever to collide with the hard, cold ground.

She heard more creaks and movement of metal above her, and then she felt something cold grab the pendant on her neck before it was torn away from her.

No, don't take my pendant away!

Jessica jerked awake with a frightening scream. She was in her sleeping bag on the stone floor in the mausoleum. She pushed against the stone bench at her back and grabbed her mini flashlight, flicking it on. Her heart felt like it would pound through her skin. She swiveled the light around, looking for anything in the night. She listened for sounds of metal creaking against metal. But she could only hear her breaths filtering out of her mouth and crickets chirping in the night.

She saw nothing around her but stone walls. She was truly alone.

She touched the pendant against her chest as she calmed down. She was safe.

"Everything's okay," she said aloud, and waited for dawn.

When the soft rays of light peered through the colored glass window, Jessica looked around her dark and stale surroundings. Since staying in the mausoleum, for the first time she saw it for what it really was—a cold, dark place for the dead. Not for someone alive.

Not for someone who *wanted* to live.

The next day during Science and Engineering class, it was time to present the Mini Bot 5000 to Mrs. Willoughby and the class. Jessica sat next to Robert at their lab table. The Mini Bot 5000 was sitting on the table between them. They'd painted some of the parts Robert's favorite color, blue. Jessica held the final written report in her hands to be turned in with the presentation.

She felt nervous, which was odd for her. She noticed Robert bouncing his leg up and down. He seemed nervous, too. They'd tested out Mini Bot 5000 a few more times, and everything had generally worked. But as they learned throughout the project, something could go wrong at any time.

During their other test runs, the Mini Bot 5000 had burned out a wire, which had to be replaced. Springs had broken and needed to be fixed. And now the final presentation was here, for better or for worse.

Jessica wanted Robert to feel better. She took something out of her book bag and held it in her hand while they listened to the other students' presentation. When the class clapped, she poked Robert in the shoulder.

He glanced at her.

"Here," she said, and opened her palm. It was her lucky rabbit's foot.

He lifted his eyebrows. "A rabbit's foot?"

"It's for luck. I know we'll do well, but it might make you feel better to have a little extra luck on your side."

He smiled as he took the rabbit's foot. "That's cool. Thanks, Jess." He dangled the short chain that it was attached to on his finger as she had done many times before.

Jessica smiled back. "You're welcome."

"I have something for you, too." He loosened the braided leather band on his wrist and handed it to her. "I'd like for you to have this."

She shook her head. "But it's yours. You always wear it."

"Now I'd like you to have it."

Jessica took the bracelet and slipped it on her wrist and tightened the band till it fit. She felt a funny warmth in her chest. "Thank you," she said quietly.

"I can't wait for tonight. Prom's going to be fun."

Jessica felt a nervous flutter in her stomach at the thought of prom.

"Robert and Jessica, you're next."

Robert stood, sliding the rabbit's foot in his pocket.

"Look, it's Ken and Zombie Barbie," the girl behind them said, and a few laughs followed.

Robert ignored them, and Jessica smiled that he didn't

let them get under his skin. He lifted the Mini Bot 5000 and they made their way to the front of the class. It took fifteen minutes to discuss their entire plan for Mini Bot 5000—the design, the components, the building of the bot, and the trials and tribulations that followed with the test runs.

"And now let's see Mini Bot 5000 in action," Robert announced.

Surprisingly, Robert handed the controller to Jessica to perform the Mini Bot 5000 presentation to the class.

Then all eyes would be on her alone.

She nearly didn't take it. She was used to being invisible, to being looked over and forgotten.

Robert gave her a reassuring smile. "You can do it," he whispered.

With a trembling hand, she took the controller. She flicked on a switch on the Mini Bot 5000 and then the remote. Robert grabbed the soda can and went to the other end of the presentation floor. She pushed the knob to move the bot forward toward Robert. Mini Bot 5000 sputtered at first as usual, then moved toward him. She stopped it right at his feet, then flicked the button so that the tray elevated.

Robert placed the can on the tray, and Jessica flicked the button so that the tray went back down. The can wobbled but stayed upright. She then backed it up and turned the Mini Bot 5000 around. She guided it to Mrs. Willoughby and raised the tray for her teacher to grab the soda.

"Well, thank you, Mini Bot 5000. I don't mind if I do," Mrs. Willoughby said. She lifted the soda, cracked open the tab, and took a sip. "Yummy." The students laughed. "A successful mini bot, you two. Great job." She praised their work as the class clapped along.

Robert smiled, and even though all eyes were on Jessica, she didn't care. She smiled back at him.

As they sat back in their seats, a girl came up to Jessica and Robert's table. Jessica automatically ducked her head, her hair sliding against her face.

"Hi," the girl said to Jessica. "I'm Tina."

Jessica lifted her head and blinked in surprise. "Oh, hi."

The girl had brown hair pulled back into a ponytail. She wore a black sweatshirt and faded jeans. Jessica noticed her in class a few times. She kept to herself and was often studying alone.

"Your bot is really cool," Tina said.

"Thank you. Um, I liked yours, too. The moving arm, right?"

"Yeah, thanks. I paired up with Blake. He's okay. Maybe next time we can work together."

Jessica glanced toward Robert, but he was talking to another student.

"Yeah, maybe we can," she said.

"Okay, see ya around, Jessica."

"Okay, bye . . . Tina."

Jessica couldn't believe it. Another student actually wanted to speak with her and possibly work with her on a project in the future. She was used to kids avoiding her, and now another student wanted to be around her. She swallowed, trying to wrap her mind around how quickly things were changing.

And she was afraid she was starting to like the changes.

After school, Jessica walked by April's hospital room. The girl was asleep. Prom was soon, but she'd wanted to come in and see how April was doing. Maybe talk to Father Jeremiah again. She passed by the nurse's station, where she overheard Nurse Macy talking to Colin, the nervous nursing assistant.

"April has a very high fever, and we've tried different antibiotics to bring it down. For some reason, nothing's working," Nurse Macy said, clearly frustrated.

"That sucks," Colin said. "She's a sweet girl. Talks with me and asks me so many questions just about my life."

"Darn it, I feel helpless when the medicines that are supposed to work don't help at all. It's frustrating. I want to help these children, not just comfort them."

Jessica gripped the pendant and wondered if she was doing the right thing by going to the prom instead of helping April. Seeing April lying in bed, pale and fragile, while she had the chance to make her better seemed so *wrong.* She had to be perfectly sure she was making the right choice.

"Oh Jessica," Nurse Macy said when she noticed her.

Jessica stepped forward. "Yes?"

"I wanted to talk to you about something important."

Jessica blinked. "Um, okay."

"It's prom night, right?"

Jessica nodded.

"I want you to have lots of fun." Nurse Macy's face blushed. "Um, and well, I tried to go by your home last night to check in on you, but there's an error on your home address you have listed with the hospital. Is it an old address?"

Jessica blinked rapidly. *Oh no.*

Suddenly an alert went off in April's room. Nurse Macy jerked her attention away.

"Call the doctor," she shouted to Colin as she rushed to April's room with two other nurses.

Jessica watched in dismay as Nurse Macy checked the machines connected to April. She demanded something of the other nurses, and Jessica watched them put a vial of medicine into April's IV. Soon April's alert turned off.

Jessica felt a pressure in her chest.

Taking a breath, she hurried to the chapel to see Father Jeremiah. April was not doing well. The prom was tonight. Her dream was still heavy on her mind. What did it all mean? Was she making the wrong choice? Was she being too selfish? Was she avoiding her destiny?

Everything was too much. The pressure to help others. The uncertainty of what to do. She just couldn't handle it.

When she got to the chapel, Father Jeremiah was speaking to a man who was crying. Father Jeremiah was whispering to him with a hand on his shoulder. Jessica walked to the first pew and sat down. She took off her pendant and held it in her hands.

Please help me understand if I am doing the right thing. I've made the wrong choices before. Could you send me a sign, please? To show me what I need to do? I feel like I just can't do this anymore. Please, I need guidance.

But no sign came to her. No answer popped into her head.

Jessica felt so alone. It was the same feeling she had felt when she knew she had changed forever. She had vowed to herself she would never feel this way again.

But it was like she was back to where she had started.

Jessica needed to get ready for prom, but she had another important question to ask Father Jeremiah. She glanced at him and saw that he was still talking with the grieving man.

She wanted to know if there really was an afterlife.

It didn't look like she would get her answer now. She left the chapel and hoped she was doing the right thing by giving herself some of her life back.

Prom night had arrived. Jessica's stomach was in knots as she walked into the prom with Robert by her side. Music seemed to bounce off the walls. Kids were chatting and laughing, dressed in pretty dresses and dark tuxedos. The dance floor looked full, and there were still more kids seated at tables. There was a corner set up to take pictures and long tables lined with snacks and drinks. Chaperones were off to the side, watching the kids dance.

Robert had given her a corsage. A pretty white rose with baby's breath, tied with a purple ribbon. Luckily, Nurse Macy had told her about the boutonniere thing, or she wouldn't have had one for him.

Some of the kids who made fun of her stared at her,

and Jessica hesitated. They likely hadn't expected Zombie Girl to go to the prom, let alone have a date.

They were probably waiting for her to do something crazy like attack them with vampire fangs or something. No, she wouldn't break out in fangs—but she might just fall on her face.

Between getting little sleep, doing all the work for the presentation, and the excitement of getting ready for prom, Jessica was exhausted. She'd gotten ready at the mausoleum instead of the hospital like she'd planned, afraid to run into Nurse Macy again and have to answer questions about where she lived. Jessica had no idea what she would tell the woman. She never really had to lie about her life because usually people stayed away from her.

In the candlelight with a small hand mirror, she had to put extra layers of makeup on her face to cover her shallow skin and the dark circles under her eyes. She'd put on some tinted eyeshadow, and she'd left her long hair down. Her nerves were practically shot, but she was determined to enjoy every minute of this prom experience. Deep within, she felt this could be her last chance to experience something very special.

"You look really pretty, Jess," Robert told her.

She glanced at him and smiled as they walked farther into the room. "Thank you. You look really nice, too." He wore a nicely fitted black tux with a light purple vest. The white rose boutonniere was pinned to his suit jacket.

"Want to dance first, or get something to drink?" Robert asked.

Jessica looked around, wondering what to do first. She wanted to soak up every part of the experience. "Let's dance first."

"All right." Robert led her to the dance floor. They squished in between couples as a slow beat began to play through the speakers. Robert put his hands around her waist, and she put her hands on his strong shoulders. He smelled of a faint cologne that he must have worn just for the dance. She realized things changed for her the moment she met Robert. Over the last few weeks, he'd slowly gotten close to her and helped her open up to him and to some of the experiences she never thought she would have again, such as making friends, being more present in her life . . . even something as simple as indulging in her favorite dessert.

She'd thought the only way to fulfill her purpose was to keep her distance from others. She thought she'd deserved to be alone for her past mistakes. But no matter how she tried to stay away from others, it hadn't worked. She'd gotten to know Nurse Macy, Robert, and now she was even making new friends like Tina.

And here she was actually at prom.

She couldn't believe this was happening.

Something good. Something special.

For her.

Maybe even though she had made mistakes in the past, she could be forgiven and be deserving of more in life. Maybe Father Jeremiah was right about being open to receiving happiness and even . . . love.

Jessica and Robert swayed back and forth to the slow

music. It was beautiful, really, even being packed in with so many kids. She could feel herself start to sweat from all the heat surrounding her. It didn't matter, though. This was a night she would always remember, so she could replay this night over and over in her mind as many times as she wanted.

"Jessica?"

Jessica looked up into Robert's eyes. It was like time stood still.

He leaned down to her ear to speak over the loud music. "Jessica, I want you to know that I really like you. Getting to know you these past few weeks has been special. When I moved here, I thought it would be the same boring experience at my other school. But when I met you, you were different. You made me feel different."

He leaned back and smiled at her.

She leaned toward his ear. "I like you, too, Robert. You've helped me . . . come out of my shell a little more. I was used to keeping to myself. I don't have a lot of friends, but you've been a good friend to me."

He smiled as she leaned back. "I'm glad I could help, and I'm happy you came to the prom with me."

"Me too."

A moment passed as they looked at each other. Then Robert leaned down toward her. He was going to kiss her.

Oh my . . .

She'd never kissed a boy before.

Her stomach fluttered. She felt sweat drip down the side of her face.

Robert's cheek glided against the dampness on her face. She felt his lips brush against hers.

Robert staggered back. "What is that?" He brushed his hand across his face, and Jessica froze.

There was dark grease on Robert's face. On his lips.

She stood frozen in horror.

Grease that was old, slick, and dirty.

And it was from *her.*

Oh no, no, no.

Something inside her cracked. As if she had been carrying within her this delicate cup of hope and dreams and happiness.

And now the cup broke, spilling out all that she had ever wanted.

"I—I'm sorry," she gushed out, frantic. "Let me help—" She reached out to Robert, trying to help him.

He jerked away. "Ugh, *filthy,*" he spat out. He swiped at his mouth, spit on the floor.

Filthy.

Jessica stepped back and knocked into someone. "Watch it," a girl snapped, then looked at her and her eyes widened. "Oh my gosh."

This was it, she thought, *this was the sign she'd been waiting for.*

Kids stopped dancing to stare at her. Some pointed at her. Others made faces of disgust. The girls from science class were laughing at her.

She'd made the wrong choice again. She shouldn't have come.

A wave of heavy darkness engulfed her.

Sounds faded in and out of her ears.

Robert. The dance. The students. The decorations. Everything drifted away as if it never existed. And that was how it was supposed to be. This world wasn't for her. It was for someone else who deserved it.

She could feel herself turning, running, as tears streamed down her face.

The blaring music disappeared. The cold night surrounded her.

And all she could do was run.

Run far, far away.

Nurse Macy was going over her patient charts at the nurse's station. She was worried about April's health. She was afraid there was no hope for the young girl. Mixed in with her worry about her patient was her worry about Jessica. She hadn't gotten a chance to talk further about the girl's address, but she wasn't going to let it go. When Jessica returned to work tomorrow, she'd sit her down and really ask her about her family. No more excuses.

She just hoped Jessica was having the time of her life at prom.

Colin walked up to her. "April is not improving. Her pulse is thready. Her vitals are weak. Fever is still high."

Nurse Macy sighed. "I know. She's the only one who hasn't made any improvement. It's not good. I just called Father Jeremiah to come and say some prayers on her behalf. It couldn't hurt. I'm open to any miracle for that young girl. I'll update her doctor right away."

Suddenly, the hospital door swung open with a loud commotion.

Nurse Macy and Colin turned their heads toward the door.

Colin sucked in air. "What the heck?"

"Jessica?" Nurse Macy called out in confusion.

Jessica looked terrible. Her face was pale. Brownish liquid streaked down her face from her forehead, eyes, and nose. The liquid had dripped down her neck onto her beautiful dress, which they had bought not too long ago.

Jessica looked wild. Crazed.

Nurse Macy stepped forward to ask her what happened but stopped in shock as Jessica ran past her. A few nuts and bolts littered behind her, scattering. They were followed by an old wrench and a rusty bike pedal that fell to the floor.

Nurse Macy's eyes widened as Jessica ran into April's room.

"We need security," Colin said from behind Nurse Macy.

Then Jessica slammed the door shut.

Nurse Macy and Colin scrambled toward the door.

"It's jammed," Colin spat out, struggling to turn the handle.

Nurse Macy hit the door with her palm. "Jessica, open the door. Talk to me, please."

Through the glass of the hospital room, she watched Jessica pull the necklace from over her head. It was the pendant she'd always seen her wear.

Then she somehow had a knife!

"Jessica!"

Jessica began to whittle away at the charm above April's bed.

"Hurry, get this door open!" Nurse Macy called out to Colin and to a security guard that had run over to help.

"I am, but she blocked the door with something," the security guard said.

Nurse Macy pounded on the glass. "*Jessica, please.* Open the door! I need to see April. Whatever happened, it's going to be okay. I can help you."

"What's going on?"

Nurse Macy turned to see Father Jeremiah. "It's Jessica. She's locked herself in April's room. We can't get in."

"Maybe I can help."

Just then, the security guard and Colin were able to push the door open, sliding whatever was blocking the door.

"Thank goodness." Nurse Macy rushed in. She spotted April still asleep in the bed.

But where was Jessica?

"Oh gross," Colin said, pointing to the floor. "How did all that get in here?"

There on the floor beside April's bed was a pile of metal pieces. Steel bars, gears, bolts, and junkyard garbage. Smelly grease dripped from the pile, as if it were blood.

"What is going on here?" Nurse Macy whispered.

"Could she have gone out the window?" Colin asked. He looked out the window but found it locked. The security guard checked the restroom.

Nurse Macy shook her head bewildered as she turned

toward the door. "Father Jeremiah . . . Jessica's gone. Just vanished. I don't understand . . . she was just *here*."

Father Jeremiah stepped into the room. He looked down at the pile of metal with a quiet sadness as if he understood something no one else could. Then he made the sign of the cross and began to pray.

In that moment, Nurse Macy heard April's heart monitor level out into a strong, healthy rhythm.

LALLY'S
GAME

IT'S TOO GOOD TO BE TRUE, SELENA THOUGHT, GRINNING AS SHE REACHED OUT AND TOOK CADE'S HAND. TURNING HIS SUV ONTO THE LONG WINDING ROAD LEADING TO THEIR NEW HOUSE, CADE GLANCED AT SELENA AND SMILED BACK AT HER. THEN HE RETURNED HIS GAZE TO THE ROAD.

A warm breeze slipped through the open passenger window and blew a few strands of Selena's long auburn hair across her eyes. She laughed and brushed them away.

She turned to look at her fiancé's handsome profile. Cade didn't notice her gaze. His eyes were on the road ahead.

How did I get this lucky? Selena asked herself.

All Selena's friends agreed that Cade was an amazing catch. He had it all.

To start, Cade was the epitome of the cliché—tall, dark, and handsome. With wavy black hair and deep-set green eyes under thick black brows, Cade had the kind of face a romance novelist would describe as "chiseled." Selena thought Cade looked like a rugged movie star. He had the prominent nose, full mouth of straight white teeth, and square chin of an action hero. He even had an enchanting dimple in that chin, and his mouth quirked in an endearing lopsided way when he grinned. He had the kind of whiskers that grew at the speed of light; even though Cade shaved every morning, his "five o'clock shadow" showed up by 10:00 a.m. It added to the "I could beat you up if I wanted to" appearance.

Fortunately, however, Cade didn't go around beating people up. He didn't have the brain or personality of an action hero. He wasn't a "man's man." Selena didn't like men like that—the men who wanted you to feel their muscles and regale you with stories of their athletic prowess. Cade was a lot more subtle than that. Yes, he was fit and played several sports, and yes, he had very fine muscles, thank you very much. But there was more to Cade than his looks.

Cade was smart and driven—he'd graduated in the top of their college class, and he had a great, high-paying computer science job lined up with a top company. He was also romantic, attentive, and funny.

As if all that weren't enough, Cade was clean and tidy and could cook. Oh yeah, and he loved his mom. Cade's mom was the reason he and Selena were moving to his hometown. Yes, his new company was located there, but he'd only applied to it after he'd suggested to Selena that they move because his mom was "getting up there" in age. Cade's mom had given birth to Cade in her late forties, so she was turning seventy this year. Cade wanted to be close to his mom to help her out if she needed it. Selena thought that was so sweet.

On top of everything else, Selena mused as she squeezed Cade's hand, Cade now had Selena, and she was an amazing catch, too. Selena grinned at her self-praise. But hey, it was true. Selena was smart and nice, and she knew men found her to be beautiful. In fact, it was her looks that had paid for her college degree. She was tall and naturally slender, and she'd modeled since she was sixteen. She'd done really well in the modeling world. Her earnings had more than covered college tuition and room and board; her combination of pale, lightly freckled skin, large hazel eyes, high cheekbones, and sensuous lips (according to her agent) was, for reasons she never fully understood, highly sought-after.

Yeah, Selena and Cade were the perfect couple. And they were going to be married in a few weeks. It was like a fairy tale, without any trolls or ogres . . . at least so far.

Sometimes in the middle of the night, Selena would

wake up suddenly. Her chest would feel tight, her skin chilly and clammy. She figured it was a mini anxiety attack, and they made her feel stupid. She'd freak out not because something was wrong but because everything was right. All Selena's friends had some kind of drama in their lives. Selena's life was sailing along perfectly. What was it they said about the other shoe? In those freak-out moments in the middle of the night, Selena knew she was waiting for that shoe to drop.

But it wasn't dropping today.

Selena pulled her gaze from Cade and looked out the open window next to her. She was delighted by what she saw.

Selena and Cade had attended college in a large metropolitan area; that was where Selena had been born and raised, too. Selena didn't hate the city she'd lived in her whole life, but she didn't love it, either. She'd always gravitated toward the countryside, to nature and small towns.

Cade's hometown wasn't exactly a small town, but it was smallish. It actually *had* been a small town until the tech company that Cade would be working for had set up its headquarters in the area. The huge complex had created hundreds of new jobs and drawn thousands of new people to the region, Cade had told Selena. New subdivisions were built. Malls showed up outside the town's original core.

Cade and Selena, however, wouldn't be living in the new areas. They'd bought a quaint old farmhouse that sat on its own five acres of meadows and apple orchards on the outskirts of the town. The pale gray two-story house (plus attic) with the massive detached garage and large front porch was a fixer-upper, but Cade and Selena thought the work would be fun. When they were done, they'd have a house perfectly suited to them.

Selena was excited to move into the house and start the renovations, but she had to wait two weeks for that. Cade was old-fashioned; they wouldn't live together until after they were married.

Cade lifted a hand from the steering wheel and pointed through the windshield. "The movers beat us here . . . barely." A trace of humor hummed through his smooth, deep voice. Cade had a great speaking voice—he could have been a disc jockey.

Selena looked ahead. A bright blue moving van was turning into the driveway that curved past the apple trees that surrounded the farmhouse she and Cade had bought together.

"I thought they had another stop to make. They must have taken the bypass," Selena said.

"And they didn't have to visit three country stores because they were 'so cute' and might have vintage clothes," Cade teased.

Selena laughed. Cade smiled at the sound. He said her laugh sounded like a cartoon princess's. Although Selena's speaking voice was low and smooth, her laugh was high-pitched and musical. "I always expect little animated birds and forest creatures to come running when you laugh," Cade had told her on their second date. That might have been when she'd fallen in love with him.

Selena playfully slapped Cade's arm. "I found two

vintage hats and a stunning homespun scarf in those stores. And I *had* to have that vintage dress. I'll write about the stores on my blog—it will be a business expense."

"That's my girl," Cade said. "Always thinking like an entrepreneur."

Selena smiled. That was another one of Cade's great qualities. He appreciated Selena's success.

In college, Selena had majored in business, and the previous year, as part of a class project, she'd started an online business—a blog and website devoted to helping women be their true selves. She created info products—e-book and audio packages that improved women's self-esteem and helped them look and feel their best. Her packages and her blog became so popular so quickly that Selena had earned enough from the whole enterprise to match Cade's contribution to the down payment for their new house (his share was an inheritance from his recently deceased great-aunt). Selena planned to continue running the business after they married; she was thrilled she'd be able to work at home. She wanted to be the consummate country bride, a happy homemaker . . . who also happened to be building an online empire.

Cade turned into their driveway. He leaned forward eagerly, his eyes bright. Selena loved seeing him so happy.

Cade was never actually *un*happy, but he leaned toward the quiet and serious side. He'd been very intense about his studies; she assumed he'd be the same about his work. He was really excited about his new job. He'd been talking about it most of the way here.

Cade pulled the SUV up beside the moving van. He turned off the engine and swiveled to look at Selena.

"Ready for this?" he asked her.

"What? Moving into our house, or getting married?"

"Both."

"I can't wait." Selena grabbed his hand and kissed his fingers.

Cade had the best hands—large and square with the faintest traces of black hair on the backs. She entwined her long, thin fingers with his thick, large-knuckled ones. She held up their hands. "Let's do this."

Letting go of Cade, Selena grinned and threw open the passenger door. She got out of the SUV and inhaled the sweet smell of the apple trees' tiny white blossoms.

"Wow!" Selena threw out her arms and spun in a circle. "I'm going to get to see these blossoms every spring!"

Cade got out of the SUV and chuckled at Selena's enthusiasm. He waved at the two muscular guys who were opening up the back of the van. The movers, Ed and Bailey, had picked up Cade's things first; then they'd come to the apartment Selena had shared with her roommate, Val, and they'd added her belongings to the van.

"I thought we'd spend the afternoon here overseeing the move, and then I'll take you to my mom's house," Cade said.

"Sounds good." Selena would be staying with Cade's mom until the wedding.

Cade came around the front of the SUV. He gave Selena a quick kiss. "You want to unlock the house? I'll go talk to the movers." Cade headed toward the two big men.

Selena grinned and started toward the porch that ran along the front of the house. She loved that porch. She couldn't wait to buy a porch swing.

Selena stood in front of the stone fireplace in the large living room just beyond the farmhouse's small slate-floored entryway. She held a clipboard, and she checked off the bureau that Ed, the larger of the two muscle-bound movers, was carrying in. "That goes in the second bedroom to the right at the top of the stairs," she told him.

"Got it," he said. He headed toward the stairs.

A couple seconds later, Bailey stepped into the house with a big brown steamer trunk propped on his shoulder. Selena scowled at the dirty and scarred old trunk with the aged leather straps and the tarnished and dented brass clasps, lock, and edging. She wrinkled her nose at the trunk's musty odor, which she could smell even from several feet away.

"What's that doing here?" she asked.

"Don't ask me," Bailey said. "I just work here." He shifted the trunk.

Selena sighed and pointed at the floor. Bailey set down the trunk a few feet from Selena and trudged back out of the house. Selena walked up to the trunk and glared at it. Frowning, she tucked her clipboard under her arm and bent over to lift the trunk. Bailey had carried it as if it wasn't that heavy.

Cade popped through the door moments after Bailey was out of sight. "They're almost finished with . . ." Cade stopped when he saw Selena in front of the trunk. His face flushed, and his jaw tightened. "What are you doing?" he snapped.

Selena cringed at the edge in his voice. His tone was sharp, and it was wrapped in what almost sounded like a snarl. Cade had never lashed out at her like that before. He'd never looked this upset before, either. She wasn't sure how to respond.

Selena decided she'd start with her best dirty look. She'd perfected the expression since childhood. She'd used it regularly on her big brother. She'd only had to pull out the look a couple times before on Cade, though—once when he'd failed to praise the chocolate chip cookies that she'd baked for him on the anniversary of their first date, and again when he'd made a snarky comment about how many shoes she had. Since then, he hadn't given her cause to glower at him . . . until now.

"What do you mean, what am *I* doing?" Selena flung back at him. "What are *you* doing? I thought we agreed to bring only our best stuff. We can afford to buy new things. We don't need old secondhand junk lying around."

Cade hurried over. He took Selena's elbow and started steering her away from the trunk. Although she didn't want to walk away from the trunk—because she wanted to open it and see what was so important that Cade would get all uptight about it—she let him lead her to the other side of the room.

Cade's face smoothed back into its normal placid lines. He took a breath. "Sorry. I didn't mean to be short with you." He gave her his trademark lopsided grin. "What we agreed to bring was our best stuff *and* our memorabilia. I'm pretty sure a lot of your boxes are filled with photos and keepsakes from your childhood."

Selena shrugged. "Yeah. But this"—she gestured at the trunk—"when I asked you about it that first night I went to your place, you said it was just an old trunk. You didn't say it was full of memorabilia. So, I figured since it was so ratty, you'd leave it behind. What's even in it?"

Cade put his arm around Selena's shoulders. He shrugged. "Oh, just some old stuff from my childhood. Keepsakes. Like we agreed to."

Selena made a face. "Can't you store your keepsakes in something more, I don't know, modern?"

"I thought you liked antiques, Miss 'I Have to Have That Vintage Dress'?"

Selena smiled. He had a point. "Okay, so not modern. How about just . . . prettier. Less . . . creepy. That thing looks like it belongs in a haunted house or something."

Cade's arm tightened around Selena for an instant. It relaxed as fast as it squeezed, so she might have imagined the brief sensation of tension in Cade's muscles.

"I promise I won't insist we use the trunk as a coffee table," Cade said. He looked down at Selena and gave her another of his irresistible grins.

Selena had gotten to know Cade's mom pretty well over the couple of years she and Cade had dated. The lady was very sweet. With graying black hair that she wore in a bob, she was much shorter than Cade's six foot two. She wasn't nearly as fit as her son, either. Cade's mom ("call me Janice, dear") reminded Selena of her own grandmother. Round-shouldered and soft bellied, Janice looked as sweet as she acted. She had a heart-shaped face with deep-set green eyes like Cade's, and her wrinkles—smile lines around her eyes and mouth—somehow added to rather than subtracted from her pleasant face. Partial to pastel polyester pants and floral blouses, Janice looked like the quintessential country momma, and it was clear she was comfortable with who she was. Selena liked that about Janice, and Selena was looking forward to spending more time with her soon-to-be mother-in-law. She knew Janice was a great cook and an even better baker (they'd spent several holidays at Janice's house), and Selena was excited about learning all Janice's culinary tricks.

Selena decided she'd ask Janice to start with the roast chicken Janice served the first night Selena was going to stay with her. How did Janice make the chicken so perfectly moist on the inside and crispy on the outside? Selena just had to know.

"Oh, it's all sleight of hand, dear," Janice said, deadpan. Unlike her son's deep voice, Janice's voice was girlish—she sounded more like a preteen than a senior citizen.

Selena blinked at her.

Janice and Cade laughed.

"She always says that when someone compliments her," Cade said, reaching out to pat his mom's liver-spotted hand.

Janice winked at Selena. "I'm just kidding, dear. I'll teach you. It's about getting the cooking temperature right . . . and a couple other secrets I'll pass along."

Selena smiled and leaned back, totally stuffed. It was a good thing she didn't plan to model anymore. Eating like this wasn't going to do her figure any good. She wasn't too worried about it, though. She planned to take long walks along all the great country roads near their new house.

Selena looked around Janice's cozy dining room. Janice lived in a sprawling white ranch-style house. According to Cade, the home used to be linked to an actual ranch that belonged to his great-grandparents, who had owned several hundred head of cattle. By the time Cade was born, though, the family had given up cattle ranching. His grandparents had sold off the bulk of the land, keeping just a few acres for privacy around the home. Cade's dad had been an attorney. He'd died of a heart attack when Cade was young.

Because Janice loved ceramic figurines, doilies, and overstuffed furniture, the interior of Janice's home was a lot fussier than Selena preferred. But it was homey, too. You felt like you could relax and be yourself in this house.

Janice stood and started gathering up dirty dishes from her oak trestle table. Selena started to help, but Janice waved her away. "Cheesecake for dessert, anyone?"

Cade's arm shot up. Janice laughed.

"I'll have a piece, and then I'm going to head back to the house," Cade said. "I'll be up early tomorrow. I want to get in a jog before work."

Janice patted Cade's arm. "That's my boy. Fit as a fiddle."

She grinned. "And starting your new job." She turned to look at Selena. "And a wedding coming up. It's all so exciting."

It sure was. Selena wanted to laugh out loud in glee. She smiled widely at Janice. "Thank you so much for letting me stay here and for helping with the wedding."

"Oh, pish posh, dear," Janice said. "It's my pleasure."

Selena had expected the two weeks she spent with Janice to be a whirlwind of wedding preparations, but it turned out that Janice had everything well in hand. Selena only had a few details to handle. She had more time to work than she'd thought she would.

Because Janice was a social butterfly with a seemingly endless number of clubs and committees, she was rarely home during the day. She was so busy, in fact, that Selena wondered why Janice needed Cade's help at all. But it didn't matter. Selena was happy to be here. She was, however, looking forward to moving into their new house.

While she was with Janice, Selena was staying in Cade's old room, which Janice hadn't changed since Cade had moved out. Selena thought it was sweet that Cade's space-themed bedspread was still on the twin bed and his constellation-patterned curtains still hung over the windows. She was touched by the bookcases stuffed with sci-fi novels and old school science, math, and computer programming textbooks. She was also amused by the collection of plush toys and action figures that coexisted on the tops of the chest of drawers and the desk tucked into the corner of the room. She was curious as well.

She'd noticed a few photo albums and scrapbooks stacked on the floor of the small closet where she hung her clothes. Cade had never shown her photos from his childhood—she hoped the albums would show her what she'd been missing.

Four days before the wedding, Selena realized she was too fidgety about her upcoming nuptials to get any work done. Janice was out. Cade was at work. Selena closed up her laptop, which she'd squeezed between several toy astronauts and a plush frog, and she stepped over to the closet door. Pulling the door open, she sat cross-legged on the floor in front of the stack of albums.

Selena reached for the first album. Brushing dust off its cover, Selena opened the leather-bound book and smiled at the photo of the gap-toothed little boy that looked up at her from the first page. Cade had been as cute as a kid as he was handsome as a man.

Selena started flipping through the photos.

The first two pages of photos were pretty normal shots of Cade with his mom and dad in front of a birthday cake. The third page, however, was a little weird.

At first, Selena didn't know what she was looking at. The photo showed little Cade in near darkness. Around him, bright-colored luminescence nearly jumped out of the picture's inky backdrop. Selena realized Cade must have been in a blacklight arena. Flipping the page, Selena saw a photo of Freddy Fazbear, the namesake of Freddy Fazbear's Pizzeria. Selena had heard of the pizza place, but Cade had never mentioned it. Strange.

A few more photos revealed that the blacklight arena

was in Freddy's Pizzaplex; in one photo, Cade was pointing up at the Pizzaplex's glowing red sign. Selena had heard of Freddy's Pizzaplex, too. It was one of the first family fun centers built in the state—a combination of arcade and indoor carnival with games and rides and food. The album had a photo of Cade in front of nearly every game and ride in the complex, but the bulk of the photos were taken in the blacklight arena. According to a huge sign at the back of the arena, the place was called Lally's Game. That was something Selena had never heard of. The place looked pretty eerie. For some reason, even just studying a photo of it made Selena shiver.

A *thud* from behind Selena startled her. She dropped the album and whipped around.

"Sorry, dear," Janice said. "I didn't mean to scare you. It's these aging legs of mine. Sometimes I get dizzy and walk right into walls." She laughed.

Janice, wearing a powder-blue polyester pantsuit, came into the room. "What have you got there, dear?"

Selena picked up the fumbled album. She rose to her feet.

"Oh, one of Cade's old photo albums," Janice said. "How fun." She crossed to the twin bed and sat. She patted the mattress. "Show me what you found."

Selena joined Janice on the bed. Sitting and opening the album, Selena inhaled the flowery scent of Janice's perfume as she flipped forward to the last few pages she'd been looking at.

The next picture in the album was yet another shot of Cade pointing happily at the Lally's Game sign. Janice tapped the sign and smiled. "Oh, my. I have such fond memories of that place."

"Freddy's Pizzaplex?"

"Well, yes, but especially Lally's." Janice ran her index finger over the picture. "It was Cade's favorite game. We couldn't get him out of the place. I think if he could have lived there, he would have." She chuckled.

Selena raised an eyebrow. The dark arena with its glowing neon-green-and-purple-and-yellow geometric designs and prehistoric-looking caves and caverns didn't look all that appealing to her. There was something . . . *off* about it, something that made her feel edgy for reasons she couldn't discern.

Janice scooted closer to Selena and turned the page. She looked at the next picture and laughed.

Selena didn't laugh. Her unsettled feeling deepened as she looked at the photo of Cade with what, at first glance, appeared to be an unfriendly version of the famous friendly ghost but at second glance was clearly a robot.

"That was Lally," Janice said, poking at the robot's round white face just above its soulless black eyes.

Selena rubbed the back of her neck. It felt like ants were crawling out of her hair.

"Lally was there to be a playmate for the kids who didn't have a friend to play with," Janice said. "Cade's best friends didn't like the game as much as he did, so he was usually in the arena by himself."

Janice was sitting right next to Selena, but for some reason, her voice sounded like it was coming from far away. Selena was so mesmerized by Lally that she felt like she'd been pulled out of Cade's old bedroom and sucked into the photo with the small, disturbing robot.

It was difficult to tell from the photo because Selena didn't know how tall Cade had been at the time, but Lally looked to be somewhere between three and four feet tall. Mostly white and smooth—with a plastic or rubber outer shell?—the bald robot had articulated arms and legs, and at each bend of its limbs, the joints were black. The same blackness joined its neck and torso. The robot's outer shell had been given some vaguely humanlike definition: it had small ears and a small nose, the faintest raised trace of eyebrows over the lidless black eyes, and some subtle muscular definition in the torso and limbs. Its mouth was a barely-upturned curve, thick-lipped.

Selena flinched when Janice turned to the next page in the album. Selena had forgotten Janice was even there. Janice didn't notice Selena's slight movement. She pointed at the next picture, in which Lally and Cade stood together. The robot was positioned so it appeared to be looking up at Cade with an expression Selena thought was vaguely hostile. No, not hostile . . . possessive.

The picture was the last one in the album. Janice rubbed her fingers over it and sighed. "One day, someone stole Lally," she said. "And that was the end of that."

Janice looked at her watch. "Oh dear. Is that the time? I was going to bake a batch of wheat rolls. Would you like to learn how to make them? Cade loves them."

Selena was still staring at the photo of Cade and Lally. She looked up at Janice. "Was Cade sad?" she asked.

Janice turned. "What do you mean, dear?"

"When Lally was taken . . . was Cade sad?"

Janice took the album from Selena and closed it. "No, dear. He was scared."

Janice crossed to the closet and replaced the album on the stack. Then she brushed her hands together briskly. "I'm going to change. I'll meet you in the kitchen, dear."

Selena wanted to ask Janice what she meant. Why was Cade scared? But Janice was clearly done with the conversation. She bustled out of the room.

Selena reached for a sweater. She was suddenly cold.

By the time Cade showed up a couple hours later, at the end of his workday, Selena's chills had passed. She was sweating when Cade strode into the kitchen and said, "Those rolls smell great!"

Learning to perfectly knead the dough had distracted Selena from her earlier fright. Seeing Cade, though, brought it back.

Selena kept her thoughts to herself during a dinner of bean soup, fresh greens, and homemade rolls. By the end of the meal, however, she was ready to confront Cade about it. She was so distracted by the memory of the pictures in Cade's old album that she couldn't look at his face without seeing the robot's face, too.

As if sensing that Selena wanted to talk to Cade privately, Janice shooed Cade and Selena out onto the deck. "I'll take care of the dishes. You two lovebirds need your private time."

Selena didn't argue with Janice. Instead, she took Cade's hand and led him out the back door. Cade laughed when she tugged him over to the big green cushioned glider at the edge of the large cedar-planked expanse that hugged most of the back of Janice's home.

"Are we going to make out?" Cade asked, squeezing Selena close as they sat.

Selena didn't resist his snuggle, but after a few seconds, she pulled away. She turned so she could sit sideways on the glider and look at Cade directly.

"Uh-oh," Cade said. "You're wearing your 'let's talk about our feelings' expression."

In spite of the tension that she'd felt since she'd looked at Cade's album, Selena smiled. "You know me so well," she said.

"And I plan to spend the rest of our lives getting to know you better," he said.

See? Such a romantic. Selena was a very lucky woman.

An image of little Cade and Lally flashed through Selena's mind. She took a deep breath and let it out.

"Why didn't you ever tell me about Freddy's Pizzaplex?" Selena asked.

Cade was gazing at her affectionately when Selena started to speak, but by the end of her question, he'd looked away from her. The easy smile on his face disappeared for an instant. When the smile returned, it wasn't as easy.

"Whatever I thought you were going to say"—Cade chuckled—"it wasn't that." His chuckle was just a bit strained.

"Well? Why didn't you ever mention Freddy's? I looked at one of your photo albums this afternoon, and it was full of shots taken there. Your mom said you loved the place, especially this freaky attraction called Lally's Game."

A muscle twitched at the corner of Cade's eye. He compressed his lips.

"You've never said anything at all about Lally," Selena pushed, "and clearly you liked the thing because it was in a bunch of the photos."

Cade shrugged. He narrowed his eyes. "Have you told me about everything you liked when you were a kid?"

Selena blinked at the defensive, throw-it-back question. She crossed her arms. "I might have forgotten a few little things, but yeah, I mostly have told you about my favorite things. And you've talked about your childhood a lot. But you *never* mentioned Freddy's or Lally's. Your mom said Lally's was your favorite game and they had a hard time getting you out of the place. That's a pretty big deal for a kid. It's strange you haven't mentioned it."

Cade looked over Selena's shoulder. The sun had just tucked itself behind the rolling hills west of the ranch house. The sky was pink. A chilly breeze began to stir the leaves of the rhododendrons that flanked the deck. A few of the bushes' bright purple blossoms blew free of their branches and danced through the air.

"Cade?" Selena prompted. "What's going on? You're acting bizarre."

Cade stood. "I just have some bad memories from that time, okay? Someone got hurt. I don't like to talk about it."

Without waiting for Selena's response, Cade turned and headed back inside the house. As he went through the door, he called to Janice . . . warmly, without a trace of the coldness that had hardened the words he'd just thrown at Selena. "Want some help with those, Mom?"

Selena's wedding day was everything she'd hoped it would be. Almost.

Although Selena's mom had wanted to throw a wedding so far over the top that it wouldn't have been able to be held on planet Earth, Selena, Cade, and Selena's dad (who was funding everything and was happy to agree that less was more) convinced Selena's mom that a casual wedding was more tasteful. Selena's brother, David, who was as good-looking as Selena was pretty but who thought jeans and a black T-shirt was "fashion," offered the winning argument: "If you don't go along with what she wants," he told their mom, "she and Cade could always elope."

Instead of the ridiculous fluffy dress Selena's mom had chosen—a dress in which Selena looked like a merengue—Selena picked a sleek vintage silk dress with a high neck, long sleeves and semi-full skirt. Rather than a veil with a twenty-foot train, she had only a small spray of flowers in her hair, which she'd arranged into an equally sleek and simple French twist. Cade wore a navy-blue suit with a white shirt and white tie. In addition to this downscaled wardrobe, they chose to use local apple blossoms and white daisies for their flowers. Selena's mom had argued for a large bridal party, but Selena and Cade had each chosen to have just their best friend stand with them. Happily smiling, redheaded Val, wearing an

A-line navy-blue cocktail dress, was Selena's attendant. One of Cade's college buddies, lanky and good-natured Greg, wearing navy-blue pants and a white shirt, was Cade's best man.

Although Selena's mom had argued for an upscale wedding venue and a fancy catered reception, she'd yet again given in to Selena's preference, which was to be married outside. Janice had offered her backyard for the wedding and reception venue. She and her army of neighborhood lady friends also organized the unorthodox, but fun and easy, potluck reception.

As Selena stood under the apple-blossom-covered arbor in the lush green garden behind Janice's home, she faced her new husband after the minister, a perpetually smiling curly-haired man, intoned, "I now pronounce you husband and wife." This was the moment—the one Selena had been envisioning for so long.

Selena looked up into Cade's hooded eyes and expected to feel nothing but the rush of love and joy she'd held in her mind's eye. Unfortunately, the reality didn't live up to her expectations. Although Selena did feel her love for Cade as he smiled down at her, and she did feel happy to be his new wife, she also felt something she never thought she'd feel on her wedding day. She felt . . . suspicious.

For the first time in the two years that she'd been with Cade, Selena didn't fully trust him. Something about his weirdness over the trunk and his fondness for the unpleasant little robot was bothering Selena.

"You may kiss your bride," the minister told Cade.

Cade leaned down and took Selena in his arms. His

embrace made her think of all their history together. It reminded her of how much she loved him. So, as she kissed him, she tucked away her nebulous distrust.

Over a hundred people attended Selena and Cade's wedding, and because they'd been instructed to "dress to have fun; don't dress to impress," everyone had a roaring good time. The food was incredible, and the local acoustic band was unexpectedly talented and played everything from bluegrass to rock to classical, which managed to make everyone happy at one point or another. Dancing wasn't one of Cade's talents (a man had to have some shortcomings); he managed to shuffle through their slow song, and he got silly and jerked around the dance floor like a man being electrocuted during the fast songs. Selena danced her heart out. She had a blast.

At the end of the reception, before Selena and Cade got in their SUV (now bedecked in streamers and tin cans and featuring a JUST HITCHED sign on the back), Selena's family came up to her to wish her well. Selena's handsome gray-haired dad, happily casual in slacks and an open-collared pale blue shirt, hugged her first. As he held her close, he whispered, "I'm so proud of you. Remember: Be your own person. Trust your instincts. Always choose joy." Selena pulled back and smiled into her dad's wet eyes. She wiped her own tears away. "I love you, Dad."

Her brother hugged her next. He, too, whispered some advice in her ear: "Don't screw it up."

When Selena's mom, who stuck to her guns and wore an expensive designer crepe gown for the wedding

(Selena had to admit it suited her lovely, tall, and regal mother), put her arms around Selena last and asked, "Are you happy?" Selena was honestly able to answer, "Yes."

By then, Selena had nearly forgotten about the odd feeling she'd had about Cade. She decided she'd just had pre-wedding jitters.

That decision was solidified during the two blissful weeks that followed.

Cade and Selena had decided to postpone their honeymoon. For one thing, Cade had just started his new job, and for another thing, they wanted to funnel their free time and their money into fixing up the farmhouse. Accordingly, they spent their wedding night in their new home. The next day was a Sunday, and they spent the day cuddled up in their new four-poster king-sized bed (their wedding present to each other), poring over design magazines and paint chips. It might not have been everyone's idea of a perfect day, but Selena felt like she was floating on a cloud.

The floating cloud, however, plummeted to Earth the next day.

Cade went off to work before 7:00 a.m. on Monday. Selena started her day more leisurely. Although Cade loved to go for runs in the morning, Selena didn't like an early rise, and she didn't like running, either, for that matter. After Cade left, she went for a long, brisk walk and when she came back, she made herself some peach spice herbal tea. Still wearing the leggings and T-shirt she'd worn on her walk (Selena loved working at home), she took the tea into her "office" at about 9:30.

Selena's office was a small spare room just off the living room. All it contained at the moment was a white metal folding table that held her laptop and a desk lamp, her soft gray tall-backed desk chair (the only piece of office furniture she'd splurged on), and stacks of file boxes. Selena had big plans for this room, which she intended to implement over the coming week. But first, she needed to do a little actual work.

Still floating in post-wedding euphoria, Selena smiled as she opened her laptop. She clicked on the icon for her website dashboard, and she began reading her most recent reader comments and responding to them.

In the third comment, the reader thanked Selena for helping to keep "old baggage" in the past. The words completely derailed Selena's plans to work . . . because they immediately made Selena think of Cade's hidden past and his unnatural reaction to her curiosity about his hideous trunk.

Selena responded to the reader's comment, but she wasn't able to concentrate on the next one. She stood. She was going to find out what was in the trunk.

Selena didn't know whether Cade's trunk had anything to do with whatever happened at Freddy's Pizzaplex, but he'd had the same strained reaction to both things. And Selena had felt the same disquieting feeling about both subjects. Something that Selena couldn't put a finger on told her that the two things were linked.

After the confrontation over the trunk in the living room on the day the movers had delivered their stuff, Cade had picked up the trunk and said, "I'll stick this in the darkest corner of the attic. You'll never have to see it again."

He'd grinned and winked at Selena, and she'd smiled back. However, their light exchange had been fake. Recalling the moment now, Selena remembered how forced the grin, wink, and smile had been.

"What if I *want* to see it again?" Selena said out loud now. She closed her laptop and stood.

Selena's tennis shoes made little squeaks against the old, uneven hardwood flooring as she strode out of her office and trotted up to the second floor. When she reached that floor, she hurried down the long hall toward the doorway to the attic. Reaching the door, she took a deep breath and yanked it open.

A puff of dust wafted into the hall, making Selena sneeze. A faintly musty smell followed the dust.

Unlike the attic in the house Selena had grown up in, which had one of those pull-down staircases, the farmhouse's attic was reached by a normal flight of stairs—albeit slightly narrower than the stairs leading from the first floor to the second. The wood risers of the stairs were warped and worn, but they were sturdy.

Selena grabbed the white-painted railing—the paint was dirty from years of use, and it was chipping. She headed up the stairs.

Although Selena had explored the attic with delight when she and Cade had toured the house before they bought it, she hadn't been back up to the slope-roofed space since they'd moved their stuff into the house. They'd agreed to have their long-term storage items put up here. Everything else was downstairs. Selena hadn't had a reason to come up here . . . until now.

If she was honest with herself, Selena had to admit that she'd been waiting for this opportunity to come up here and look in Cade's trunk. Even distracted as she'd been by the wedding, she'd mentally put finding out what was in the trunk on the top of her to-do list. The mystery of it was chafing at her.

Selena got to the top of the stairs, and she reached for the string pull for the single exposed bulb that lit the attic. She yanked on the string. Bright white light joined the yellow glow of the sun streaming in through dormer windows on either end of the big space.

Because they hadn't yet accumulated a lot of stuff that needed long-term storing—just a few boxes of keepsakes and photo albums, a stack of luggage, and several plastic storage bins filled with holiday decorations (Selena loved holidays)—the attic was still pretty wide-open. Just a couple dozen boxes were stacked at the south end of the space.

Selena looked around, taking in the low crossbeams, the insulated underside of the roof, the aged gray wood floor, and the murky glass of the paned windows. She and Cade had plans to finish the attic and turn it into a big rec room . . . and maybe one day, it could be a playroom for their future kids. A lot of work would go into that project. But for now, at least the attic was functional as storage.

Selena strode over to the stacks of boxes. Cade must have put the trunk behind them.

Or not.

Behind the boxes, Selena found only more boxes. The trunk wasn't there.

She frowned and turned in a circle. Given that the attic had no closets or hidden rooms, it was obvious the trunk wasn't where Cade had said he was going to put it.

He'd lied.

Selena ground her teeth. She felt her shoulders tighten. All her suspicions, which she'd tucked away successfully since that moment during the wedding, flooded back in. Her husband was keeping something from her.

Or had he gotten rid of the trunk after all?

Selena would bet big money that he hadn't.

Huffing in annoyance, Selena left the attic and trotted back down the stairs. She closed the door to the attic and stood with her back to it. She looked up and down the hall. Where had Cade stashed that trunk?

Well, if it was in this house, Selena was going to find it. She closed the door to the attic and thought for a moment.

Where would he put it?

The garage, she decided. That's where she would have put it if she'd been Cade.

The garage was more Cade's domain than it was Selena's. It was a three-car garage, and he planned to turn one-third of it into a workshop. The other two stalls would be for their vehicles.

Although Cade had a lot of tools and athletic equipment and gardening stuff, there wasn't so much of it that it could bury a trunk. It only took about fifteen minutes of poking around the garage to determine that the trunk wasn't there.

Now what?

Selena returned to the house.

The farmhouse wasn't huge—it was only about two thousand square feet, with three bedrooms and one and a half bathrooms. In all, the home had five closets plus a pantry.

Selena started in the pantry. She was pretty sure the trunk wasn't there because she'd been in and out of the room several times . . . but it could have been buried under boxes of pots and pans she hadn't opened yet.

It wasn't.

Selena moved on to the coat closet. No luck. She tried the linen closet, the closet in their room (again, she didn't expect to find it there and didn't), and the closet in the room they were going to set up for guests. No trunk.

The last closet was in what was now a completely empty room. They hadn't decided on what this room would be, so they'd just closed it up for now. Selena hadn't been in it at all since the day they'd made their offer on the house.

The door to the empty room creaked when Selena pushed it open. The sound was so reminiscent of the soundtrack of a scary movie that Selena wouldn't have been surprised to find the trunk sitting right inside the door, opening like the gaping maw of a demon ready to . . .

Selena stepped into the room. It was empty.

Setting her jaw, Selena marched across the room and jerked open the closet door. She frowned. Although the closet's hanging rod was empty and the shelf above it was bare, beneath the rod and the shelf was a stack of boxes.

This closet should have been as empty as the room. Why were there boxes in it?

Selena reached for a box. She lifted it and practically tossed it over her head. It was so light that her lift was overkill. She shook the box. It was empty.

Selena picked up the next box and the next. Every box was empty. Why would Cade have filled this closet with empty boxes? They'd agreed to break down the boxes for recycling.

There was only one reason to stack up empty boxes. They'd been used as a makeshift screen . . . to hide something.

Heat beginning to pulse in Selena's ears, she started tossing empty boxes out of the closet. Eight empty boxes—she threw them onto the vacant room's wood floor. Then she looked at a pile of blankets behind the boxes. What were the blankets doing in here? They should have been in the linen closet.

There was also only one reason for the stack of blankets. They created a nice thick cloak; they, too, were meant to hide something.

Emitting a growl of anger, Selena threw aside the blankets. And there it was.

The trunk squatted in front of her. Its two clasps and its centered lock looked not unlike a grumpy face looking up at her. A grizzled, grumpy face.

Selena didn't waste any time. She dropped to her knees. She undid the clasps with two loud metallic clicks.

Then she tried to open the lock. But it wouldn't open. It was, well, locked.

Where would Cade keep the key?

Selena sat back on her heels. The key could be anywhere.

Selena peered at the lock. Could she pick it?

Selena gave the trunk a dirty look, then stood and strode out of the room. She trotted along the hall and jogged down the stairs. She ducked into her office. Sitting, she opened her laptop and got on the internet. Her fingers were poised over the keyboard, preparing to type in "how to pick a steamer trunk lock," but then she dropped her hands. She closed the laptop.

To heck with it. She didn't want to mess around with learning how to pick a lock.

She'd be better off breaking the lock. Selena got up and left her office.

It took just a few minutes to return to the garage and get some tools. Not sure what she'd need, Selena grabbed a hammer, a crowbar, and a couple of screwdrivers. Once she had them, she returned to the house, ran back up the stairs, and strode into the third bedroom. She dropped to the floor in front of the trunk.

Selena had never needed to open a steamer trunk before, so she didn't know what she was doing. Maybe she should have found a video about prying open a trunk before just assuming it would be a breeze. She discovered quickly that the crowbar and hammer weren't helpful. Pounding and prying with the large tool did little more than make a lot of noise and put a few more jagged tears in the filthy brown duck cloth that covered the trunk's wood slats.

When Selena abandoned the larger tools, though, and picked up the screwdrivers, she had more luck. She finally popped the lock free from the trunk by using a two-pronged prying attack with both screwdrivers.

When the lock pinged loose from the trunk and clattered to the floor, she dropped the screwdrivers and did a little fist pump. "Yes!" she crowed.

Eagerly, she put her hands on both sides of the lid. She started to lift it.

From downstairs, a *thud* told Selena the front door had just closed. She heard footsteps, Cade's footsteps.

Cade—her conniving, sneaky husband—was home. And boy, was he in trouble.

Her anger trumping her curiosity, Selena let go of the trunk's lid. She leaped to her feet and ran out of the room. She raced down the stairs to confront her lying husband.

Cade looked up from shaking water out of his hair when Selena reached the bottom of the stairs. "Boy, it's really coming down out there," Cade said. "Thought I'd come home and have lunch with my beautiful wife, and halfway here, the sky decided to try to drown me."

Selena glanced out the window. It must have started raining while she was getting the trunk unlocked. She hadn't even noticed.

Selena looked back at Cade. She saw that his dark green polo shirt and his khakis were drenched.

Normally, Selena would have made a joke about

getting him out of his clothes, but she didn't feel like joking. She didn't care how soaked he was.

Selena clenched her fists against her hips. "Why didn't you put the trunk where you said you were going to put it?"

Cade wiped his face and looked at Selena. "What?"

"The trunk. You didn't put it in the attic. You *hid* it behind empty boxes and blankets. Why did you do that?"

Cade's face went so stony that it really could have been chiseled. "Did you open it?"

Selena frowned at him. She didn't answer his question.

Cade rushed over to Selena. His sopping loafers made squishy slapping sounds on the wood floor.

He grabbed her arms. "Did you open it?" he repeated. This time, he threw out the words so fast that they ran together.

"You didn't answer my question," Selena said.

Cade gave Selena a little shake. "Did you open it?"

Selena grimaced as Cade's fingers tightened on her arms. She jerked out of his grasp and stepped away from him.

"Did you open it?!" he repeated. This time the words were spaced apart: "Did . . . you . . . open . . . it?" His tone was low, almost threatening.

"No!" Selena barked. "I was about to, but I heard you coming home and—"

Cade didn't wait for her to finish. He brushed past her and pounded up the stairs. Selena gaped at him for an instant. Then she shook off her surprise and ran after him.

Cade got to the third bedroom seconds before Selena caught up to him. By the time she did, he was on his knees in front of the trunk. Taking a deep breath, he lifted the trunk's lid.

Selena stepped behind Cade and looked down into the trunk. She exhaled her pent-up breath.

The trunk was empty. Completely empty.

"No," Cade breathed. He lifted his head and looked around. He was ashen. His gaze darted around the room. His eyes moistened. For a second, Selena thought he was going to cry. Then he wiped a hand over his face and looked back down at the empty trunk.

Selena didn't know what she'd expected to find in the trunk, but seeing it empty had flooded her with relief. She still didn't know what the deal was with Cade and the trunk, but at least it didn't contain something horrible.

"I'm so sorry," Selena said.

Selena put her hand on Cade's shoulder. Through his wet shirt, she could feel his shoulder trembling. In spite of being drenched, he didn't feel cold, so she assumed he was shaking because he was so angry with her. She had, after all, not only made it clear she didn't trust him, she'd violated his trust, too. She'd poked into his private stuff. She'd have been furious if he'd done that to her. Not that she had anything to hide.

"I'm really, really sorry," she said. "I just . . . oh, I don't know. It just bugged me, why you were so secretive about that stupid trunk. But I'm so sorry. I should have trusted you. I shouldn't have . . ."

Cade stood. He turned and wrapped his arms around Selena. "It's okay," he said. "It's okay."

Selena wasn't sure it was okay. Pressed against his

wet-shirt-covered chest, she could feel his racing heart, and she felt the tightness in the muscles of his arms and shoulders as she returned his embrace. She also smelled something she'd never smelled on Cade before—it was the odor of rancid sweat. She stepped back and looked at his face. His forehead was moist. He'd wiped away the rain, so it wasn't that. It was perspiration. He was scared. That was what she was smelling—it was the stench of fear.

Selena knew it wasn't okay. No matter what Cade said. She didn't discover how not okay it was, though, until that night.

Cade had settled himself pretty quickly after he'd closed the trunk and stuck it back in the closet. He'd ignored the scattered empty boxes and the blankets. It was as if he didn't see them. More likely, he didn't want to explain why he'd gone to such lengths to hide an empty trunk.

Selena was so reassured by the empty trunk that she didn't press Cade about why he'd hidden it the way he had. Instead, she'd said brightly, "I'll make us tuna sandwiches."

Cade had changed his clothes. Coming downstairs in another pair of khakis and a dark blue polo shirt (Cade's wardrobe was a little limited), he had made small talk about his work while they ate. Selena had told him about her morning walk. The conversation had sounded okay, with all the right bits of humor, but it hadn't been quite right. There was an undertone to their words, one that they both ignored.

Cade had returned to work after lunch. Selena forced

herself to put the whole trunk business out of her mind. She had to get some work done, too.

Dinner was a little more normal than lunch had been. She'd tried a new pasta recipe, and Cade had said he loved it. He'd even had a second helping.

Only the barest trace of tension had remained between them by the time they'd gotten ready for bed. The tension returned, though, when Cade gave Selena a peck on the cheek and told her he was exhausted and needed to go right to sleep. Usually, they cuddled before settling in, snuggling together and talking drowsily about their plans for the next day. Not that night. Cade got under the covers and closed his eyes. Selena was wide-awake, but she got into the bed next to him, and she turned out the light.

They lay next to each other—not touching, not talking. Selena listened to Cade's even breathing. He was pretending to be asleep, but he wasn't. There was an outgoing hiss in his breath when he was really asleep. Selena didn't hear the hiss.

Selena, who practiced meditation and yoga, was more adept at feigning sleep. She slowed her breathing and relaxed all her muscles. She knew she appeared to be asleep, but she wasn't.

Selena wasn't sure how long she focused on her breathing before she heard Cade stir. She felt the covers lift—a cool air current fluttered against her bare arms. The mattress shifted. Cade was up. The floor creaked. He was moving away from the bed.

Selena just barely opened her eyes. She shifted her head slowly and quietly.

Because they hadn't yet agreed on a color scheme for the bedroom, the two paned windows that looked out over the backyard were covered only with the flimsy sheers that the previous owners had left behind. The sheers did little to block out light. Now they let in the radiance of a three-quarter moon in filmy shimmers that sprayed across the room. Selena could clearly see Cade in that gleam.

Selena watched as Cade got down on his knees. His head disappeared below the level of the mattress. He seemed to be looking under the bed.

Cade raised his head. Selena closed her eyes. She listened to his footsteps move away from the bed. She opened her eyes again.

Cade was moving around the room slowly. It looked like he was searching for something. His head swiveled left and right and back again as he moved from his side of the room to hers. On her side, he opened the closet door. He looked into the closet—pushing back clothes—for a few seconds, then shut the door.

Selena closed her eyes again when Cade turned around. She concentrated on her easy breathing as Cade rounded the bed and got back under the covers. This time, Cade's breathing settled into his familiar hissing rhythm a few minutes after he lay down. It took Selena a while before she joined him in sleep.

And that sleep didn't last long.

Cade's footsteps woke Selena. Lying on her side now, she glanced at the clock. It was only an hour since they'd first turned out the lights. Cade was on the prowl again.

Listening intently, she could tell he was going through the same searching routine.

Selena debated whether to turn on the light and ask Cade what he was doing. Before they'd moved into this house—before she'd found out about his peculiar attachment to the trunk and his mysterious past at Freddy's, Selena would have met the issue head-on. She wouldn't have hesitated to ask Cade what he was doing. Now she knew even if she did that, she wouldn't get an answer. And she wasn't up to dealing with any more of Cade's evasiveness just yet.

Cade got back in bed, and he returned to sleep. So did Selena.

They repeated this process three more times that night. Come morning, Cade looked wiped out when he got up to go for his run. Selena was so exhausted that she went back to sleep until Cade returned from his run. She pretended she was still asleep while he showered and got ready for work. She didn't get out of bed until she heard his SUV head down the driveway.

Selena put up with Cade's nocturnal paranoia for nearly a week before she finally had to ask him what was going on. By then, she was dragging from lack of sleep. She was fed up.

On the seventh night that Selena woke up to see Cade looking under the bed, she sighed heavily and leaned over to turn on the ginger jar lamp on her nightstand.

Cade's head shot up. His hair disheveled, he blinked into the sudden illumination. He looked like a little kid caught in the act of some mischief.

Selena scooted into a sitting position. "What exactly are you doing?" she asked.

Cade blinked again. "What do you mean?" he asked inanely.

Selena pulled the covers up and crossed her arms over them. "Don't play dumb. You know what I mean. You've been jumping in and out of bed like a jack-in-the-box for the last week. What's going on? You act like you're checking for the boogeyman."

Cade rubbed his eyes and made a face. Sighing, he pushed himself up and sat on the edge of the bed.

Selena stared at his broad shoulders and at the way his hair curled behind his ears. She loved those curls. "Cade?"

Cade turned, then slipped under the covers with her. She lay back and shifted so she could look at him. He lay down, too, facing her.

Selena reached out and touched Cade's cheek. It was rigid and cold. She looked at the dark circles under his eyes; they'd been there since the night he'd started acting paranoid.

Cade reached up and caught her hand. He kissed her knuckles. "I never wanted to tell you about any of this. I just wanted to forget it. But now . . ."

"Cade, what is it? What's going on?"

Cade took a deep breath. He opened his mouth, then closed it.

He pulled away from her. "Sorry. I need to stand for this."

Selena's stomach lurched. What was he going to tell her?

She sat up again, but she wrapped herself in the comforter. Even though the room's temperature was mild, she felt icy.

Cade began to pace around the room. "Mom told you that someone stole Lally, but that isn't true," he said.

He glanced at Selena. She didn't say anything. She concentrated on composing her face into an expression of calm nonjudgment.

"What happened," Cade went on, "was that they were doing renovations in the Pizzaplex, and a construction scaffolding collapsed during a round of Lally's Game. The collapse punched a hole in the game's exterior wall." Cade stepped over to the window and looked out into the night. The moon was close to full now. Its silvery radiance put Cade in a spotlight.

"The auditorium was evacuated, and Lally's was closed down because Lally went missing," Cade went on. "It was assumed he'd been stolen."

"But you said that's not what happened," Selena said.

Cade glanced over at her. He shook his head, then turned back toward the window. "For weeks after the Lally's Game arena was closed, I kept seeing Lally. I saw him everywhere."

He and *him*, Selena thought. Not *it*.

"I saw him on top of my shelves one day," Cade said. "One afternoon, he was on my desk, behind my toy astronauts. Once, I parted the coats in my closet, and I saw Lally standing there at the back of the closet, looking out at me. I saw him once in the bathroom, behind the shower curtain. Several times, I spotted him in the backyard. He was always hiding, like he was playing a perpetual game of hide-and-seek."

Goose bumps crept up Selena's arms. She rubbed them.

"Whenever I spotted him, he was always frozen on the spot, always smiling that half smile he had." Cade stopped talking. He rubbed his own arms as if he had goose bumps, too.

Selena cleared her throat. "Was someone playing a joke on you?"

Cade turned. His expression was resigned. "I wish. No. Lally followed me home."

Selena's breath caught. Her heart started thumping so hard in her chest she was sure Cade could hear it.

"Lally messed with me for weeks before I finally stopped him." Cade gave Selena a slightly triumphant grin. "You know Mom's sewing room?"

Selena nodded.

"One day when she was at one of her meetings, I took everything out of that room. It wasn't much then. She just had the sewing machine on the table, that dummy she pins her patterns on, and a few plastic storage bins. I emptied the room, and I dragged the trunk into the room. I figured Lally wouldn't be able to resist hiding in the trunk."

Selena bit her lip and remained silent.

"I waited an hour," Cade said. "Then I ran into the room, and I locked the trunk. I trapped him."

Selena frowned. "Did you look in the trunk to be sure he was there?"

Cade shook his head. "I didn't want to risk him getting back out. I just locked it. I knew he was inside."

Selena gazed at the man who up until this moment she'd thought was one of the smartest people she'd ever met. Cade was a programming genius, and he could talk about almost any subject. His mind was sharp, and his logic was impeccable. Usually.

The only thing Selena could conclude about what Cade had just said was that some part of his psyche was stuck in his childhood. He'd been so traumatized by the destruction of his favorite game that he'd created an elaborate fantasy around it. That had to be it.

Obviously, Cade hadn't "trapped" anything. He'd locked an empty trunk. But in his childhood fantasy, he'd convinced himself that his tormenter had been contained. It was his confidence that he'd locked up Lally that made his fear of the robot go away. That was why he stopped having hallucinations about Lally. He'd obviously been hallucinating. There was no other explanation.

Cade returned to the bed. He sat down and rotated toward Selena. "Say something."

Selena took a breath. Then she laid out her theory. She finished with a story from her own childhood. "My best friend, Zoey—you remember me talking about her—went through a phase when we were in first grade. She was sure this big purple monster was living under her bed. I mean, she was *sure* of it. She talked about it all the time. Eventually, her parents did something similar to what you did. They said they were laying a trap for the monster, and they 'caught'"—Selena put air quotes around the word—"the monster in a big box. After that, Zoey was fine. The same thing happened to you. When a child is convinced that something is trapped and can't hurt them anymore, the fear of it disappears."

Cade started shaking his head in the middle of Selena's story. By the end he was shaking his head so hard that his hair was whipping into his eyes. "Lally isn't an imaginary purple monster. He's *real.* And he was in that trunk. Before you unlocked it."

Selena didn't miss Cade's use of the present tense. *"Lally isn't."* Not *"Lally wasn't."*

Selene decided to set this troubling detail aside for the moment. It was more than she could deal with.

She scooted across the bed and took Cade's hand. "Cade, honey, nothing was in that trunk. You were a little boy, a traumatized little boy, and you reassured yourself by telling yourself Lally was locked into the trunk. That's why you stopped seeing it. It's basic psychology."

Cade didn't respond. For several seconds, he was frozen, staring at the floor.

Finally, Cade reluctantly squeezed Selena's hand. "We need to get some sleep." He got under the covers. "Turn off the light," he said.

Selena opened her mouth to object. She knew Cade was rejecting her explanation. But she was tired, and she didn't want to think about it anymore. She turned off the light and lay down. Cade scooted over and wrapped her in his arms, spooning her.

Selena forced herself to concentrate on Cade's familiar warmth. And she made herself ignore the frantic pace of his beating heart, which she could feel against her back.

Even after Cade's heart rate slowed and he settled into sleep, Selena once again remained awake for a long time.

The next couple of weeks passed relatively uneventfully. On several nights, Selena and Cade spent the evening with Janice. They helped her with chores and had dinner with her. If they weren't with Janice, Cade worked late. He worked so late that he missed dinner. He'd come home just before ten or so. They'd have a cup of tea or hot chocolate, talk about their day, and then go to bed.

Both Selena and Cade were sleeping fitfully, but they were sleeping. If Cade was getting up during the night, Selena didn't hear him. The dark circles under his eyes, though, didn't go away.

Selena kept herself busy during the day with both work and renovations. The first week after Cade told her about Lally, Selena threw herself into setting up her home office. She refinished the hardwood floor and painted the walls a mossy green. Hanging curtains in stripes of gray and the same green as the walls, she then went out and found the perfect rug, desk, credenza, and new set of filing cabinets. She hung her favorite prints on the walls, and she declared the office done.

Once she was finished with the office, Selena demolished the half bath. It felt great to swing a sledgehammer over and over. Slamming heavy steel against porcelain tiles was deliciously cathartic. Over the weekend after she destroyed the bathroom, Selena and Cade tiled the floor and installed a new toilet, vanity, and sink. They worked from sunup to sundown both days. Was there something a little frenetic about their pace? Probably. But neither of them mentioned it.

After they finished the half bath, Selena turned into the eccentric painting lady. After they agreed on a pale taupe color for the walls, with white trim, she painted the entire main floor. When she was done, she and Cade went on a marathon furniture shopping spree, purchasing an antique cherry dining room set, a navy-blue sofa and love seat, a navy-blue rug with a cream-and-taupe geometric pattern, an oak coffee table and two matching end tables, and a pair of antique brass lamps for the end tables. Selena found the perfect taupe-and-dark-blue-tweed drapes for the living room, and then she feverishly bought throw pillows and art. She spent several hours arranging and rearranging the furniture, finally settling on a configuration that put the sofa and love seat in the middle of the room. She positioned them so they flanked the fireplace. The dining room and living room were done by the end of the month.

The kitchen was going to require a professional, so they hadn't tackled that yet. However, with most of the main living areas complete, Selena decided it was time to have some people over.

Cade had made many new friends on the job. On the few nights he didn't work late, he and Selena were invited to several dinners so he and Selena could get to know Cade's new coworkers and their spouses. Between these people and the friends Selena was making on her walks and during her shopping trips, they were developing an enjoyable social network.

"Let's have the Petersons, the Taylors, and the Lees over for dinner this weekend," Selena suggested one night as they cuddled on the sofa, sipping hot chocolate. "We owe them all dinners."

"We 'owe' them?" Cade said. He grinned at Selena. "Did I miss something? Did we sign a tit-for-tat contract when we had dinner at their houses?"

Selena lightly smacked his thigh. "You know what I mean."

"Yes, I do, Miss Etiquette."

Selena rolled her eyes. "I'm thinking something casual. It's warm enough. We could barbecue."

"Sure," Cade said. He set down his mug and put his arm around Selena. "That sounds fun."

On nights like this, Selena could almost convince herself that everything was fine. She could almost forget about the trunk and about Lally. Almost.

The night of the barbecue, they had perfect weather. It was warm, and the sky was full of sparkling stars that looked like they'd been hung above their heads like party decorations.

After a feast of burgers, macaroni salad, green salad, chips, and corn on the cob followed by homemade brownies (Janice's recipe; Cade said they tasted just like his mom's), the four couples settled around the gas firepit

Selena had installed just days before the get-together. They all reclined on the plush navy-and-cream-striped patio chairs she'd bought the day before.

"How about charades?" Selena asked.

Grace Peterson, a petite woman with short-cropped blonde hair, popped out of her chair. "I want to be on Hugh's team." She poked her husband, Ron, and made him change places with her.

Ron, an unusually pale guy with long brown hair, rolled his eyes as he good-naturedly gave in to his wife's game of musical chairs. He noticed Selena's questioning look. "Hugh is a film and literature buff," he explained.

"More like a trivia nut," Hugh Taylor's wife, Theresa, said. A tall, broad-shouldered redhead, Theresa dwarfed her short, bald husband. But appearances aside, they appeared to be a perfect match. It was impossible to miss that they were crazy about each other.

Selena grinned. "Well, then I want to be on Hugh's team, too."

Everyone laughed.

Grace stood. "I've got one."

Hugh and Selena, and their other teammate, Ava Lee, an athletic brunette, looked up at her. When Grace made the universal sign for "movie," Hugh winked at Selena and Ava. They grinned.

Grace held up six fingers.

"Six words," Selena said unnecessarily.

Grace held up one finger.

"First word," Ava said.

Grace nodded. Then she shook her head. She held up one finger again.

Selena frowned, confused.

"Point?" Hugh asked. He leaned toward Selena. "The clue is the one finger."

"*Point Break!*" Selena shouted.

Cade snorted out a laugh. "That's just two words, sweetie."

Selena blushed.

Grace shook her head. She started lifting and lowering her arms as if she was flying.

"*The Birds*," Selena blurted. She blushed deeper the second the words were out of her mouth. Then she laughed. "Ignore me. I'm math-challenged."

Everyone else laughed, too.

Grace chewed on her lower lip. Then her eyes lit up. She bared her teeth and shifted her gaze to the far left. She looked deranged.

Again, Selena shouted without thinking. "*The Shining*." She was pretty pleased with herself for realizing Grace was mimicking the star actor's crazed expression in that movie.

Everyone laughed.

Selena clapped a hand over her mouth. She shook her head, then dropped her hand and laughed, too. "I really can't count, can I?"

She looked over at Hugh. He smiled at her. Then he calmly said, "*One Flew Over the Cuckoo's Nest*."

Grace clapped and rushed over to give Hugh a high five.

Selena shook her head. "Sorry for being so dense."

Ava laughed. "It's the adrenaline. Who has time to count words? I almost said *The Shining*, too; you just beat me to it."

Selena was relieved that no one was making her feel stupid for blurting out two-word answers to a six-word clue.

Ron stood and began acting out a clue for his team.

They played three rounds of charades—Hugh was a walking trivia encyclopedia, so he easily guessed whatever his teammates acted out. After the first round, Selena kept her mouth shut, to avoid further embarrassment. But her team soundly beat Ron's team, which included Theresa, Cade, and Ava's husband, Marshall.

Finally, Ron threw up his hands. "I give up. We need to play something else." He picked up his plastic mug and looked into it.

Selena stood. "Would you like another cream soda?"

Ron glanced at the big ice-filled bowl that held the canned drinks. "I think I drank them all."

Selena laughed. "We have more out in the fridge in the garage. I'll go get some."

"You sure?" Ron asked. "I can drink something else. I don't want to be a bother."

"No bother," Selena assured him.

Ava tapped Marshall. "Why don't you go get your guitar from the car, sweetie? We can play Name That Tune."

Hugh groaned. Ava winked at Selena. "Music is the dark hole in Hugh's trivia-verse."

Selena grinned. "I'm pretty good at coming up with song titles."

"Hurry back, then," Ava said. "We'll keep the same teams. Maybe you can carry Hugh."

"I'm hurrying," Selena said, chuckling.

What a fun night, she thought, as she headed around the house to the garage. She was really glad she'd suggested it.

Selena hadn't had much one-on-one time with Cade during the evening, but she'd been watching him. He'd been at ease, laughing and talking easily. He seemed like his old self. What a relief.

Pushing open the back door to the garage, Selena flipped on a light. They'd run out of bulbs with the right wattage, and they'd had to substitute wimpy 60-watt bulbs in the overhead lights. The bulbs didn't throw enough light to brighten the whole garage. Much of the space sat in pockets of dingy darkness.

Selena went past the SUV and their new small red pickup (they'd driven it home the previous week). She strode toward the extra fridge tucked against the wall.

The fridge was flanked by several stacks of boxes Cade hadn't had time to unpack yet. His workshop space was still waiting to be set up. Next to the boxes, the lawn mower, Weedwacker, blower, bush trimmer, hoses, and a few other yard maintenance odds and ends were in a tangle that Cade promised he'd "sort out" soon. Next to this jumble, a shop vac sat on top of a metal workbench that Cade hadn't yet put into place.

As Selena reached the fridge, her gaze skimmed over the shop vac. She started to open the fridge door. Her hand froze. She flicked her gaze back toward the shop vac.

Selena's heart catapulted into her throat. She gasped.

Next to the shop vac, a small white robot with black eyes stood upright.

It was Lally. It had to be. It looked just like the robot in the photos.

The robot didn't move, but it was facing Selena. She felt like it was watching her.

For several seconds, Selena was frozen. While her heartbeat galloped and invisible mites crawled along her arms, she stared at Lally in shock.

When Lally remained motionless, Selena whipped open the fridge and grabbed a six-pack of cream soda. Letting the fridge door slam, she looked toward the shop vac again. In the seconds it took her to open and close the fridge and look that way again, she debated whether she wished the robot would be gone or still be there. Which would be worse?

The robot was still there.

Selena turned and raced back through the garage. Slamming the door behind her, she ran around the house, slowing her pace only when she was within view of her guests.

Back near the gas firepit, she handed a can of soda to Hugh and put the rest of the sodas in the bowl of ice. She casually walked over to Cade.

Marshall was tuning up his guitar. Everyone else was chatting. Cade was having a conversation with Ava about some coding issue they were facing in the project they were working on together.

Selena stepped up beside Cade and put a hand on his arm. She couldn't miss the fact that her hand was trembling.

She looked at Ava. "Sorry to interrupt, but I need to steal him for a minute."

Cade raised an eyebrow in question.

"I, uh, need you in the garage a minute, honey," Selena told him.

"Everything okay?" Cade asked.

"Uh, yeah. Just . . ." She gave Ava a tight smile. "Sorry. I'll bring him right back."

Ava smiled. "No problem." She turned toward her husband.

"What is it?" Cade asked as Selena grabbed his hand and pulled him toward the garage. She was trotting. He stumbled over a tree root. Then he, too, started jogging, picking up on her urgency.

Selena hesitated at the garage door.

"Are you going to tell me what's wrong?" Cade asked.

Selena didn't answer him. She took a deep breath and opened the door.

The garage lights were still on. She'd left them on purposefully. She hadn't wanted to turn them off before she was out of the garage, not with that *thing* in there. The fact that it wasn't moving when she left had done very little to lower her panic level.

Selena stepped into the garage and pointed toward the shop vac. "Look," she said. After she spoke, she got up the courage to do the same thing she was asking Cade to do.

"What am I looking at?" Cade asked.

Selena blinked at the empty spot on the workbench next to the shop vac. The robot was gone.

"It was there," she said.

"What was there?" Cade asked. "Did a raccoon get in here? I shooed one away last week."

Selena shook her head. She quickly scanned the garage.

The robot wasn't in sight, but that didn't mean anything. The garage had way too many places to hide.

Selena groaned. Now she was getting as paranoid as Cade was.

Cade stepped in front of Selena. "I'll ask again. What's going on?"

Selena looked up at him. She swallowed. "I . . . I saw . . . I saw Lally, I mean, I think it was Lally. It was a white robot that looked exactly like the one in the picture and—"

"Where'd you see him?" Cade interrupted.

Selena pointed. "Next to the shop vac."

Cade strode across the garage. He looked all around the workbench and behind the boxes on either side of the fridge. Then he turned and began searching the rest of the garage.

Selena stood near the door, poised for reasons that had no foundation in logic. To run. Her mind was a tangle of incoherent thoughts. A funny white-noise-like sound buzzed in her ears. What was going on here?

Cade returned to Selena. A furrow bunched the skin between his brows.

"I didn't imagine it," Selena said.

"I didn't say you did," Cade said.

"But—" Selena began.

Cade took her hand. She didn't resist when he pulled her out of the garage and closed the door behind them. He, too, left the lights on.

"We have guests," Cade said. "They're going to be wondering what we're doing."

Selena nodded. He was right. Now wasn't the time to talk about what she'd seen. It wasn't the time to think about it, either.

They rounded the corner of the house, and Selena pasted on her happy hostess smile. "Sorry about that," she called out.

"A little rodent issue," Cade lied.

Selena noticed how natural the lie sounded. But she didn't take the time to think about that, either.

The day after the dinner party, Cade was gone when Selena woke up. She found a note on his pillow.

The note, she knew immediately, contained another lie: "Sorry. Got called into work. Love you."

Cade never got called into work on a Saturday. He was merely avoiding her. He didn't want to talk about what had happened.

Well, neither did she. She wanted to forget about it.

Selena got up and looked outside. The day was bright, but she didn't feel like taking a walk. What *did* she feel like doing?

The truth was that however much she wanted to forget what had happened, Selena was rattled by it. Really, really rattled.

Selena got up, pulled on her dark blue terrycloth robe, and went down the hall. What she needed was a long, hot bath.

As Selena shuffled toward the bathroom, she thought about the master suite they intended to have. They planned to knock out a wall and steal some space from the guest bedroom so they could create an en suite bathroom for the master bedroom. They'd just discussed, a couple days before the get-together, whether to tackle that or the kitchen next. She was thinking the en suite should come first.

Selena went into the bathroom. She left the bathroom door open. She always left the bathroom door open when she took a bath, even when Cade was home. She didn't like steaming up the room.

Turning on the tap at the end of the claw-foot tub under the window, Selena ran the water until it got hot. She adjusted the temperature, put in the drain plug, and poured some muscle-relaxing bath salts into the water. The bath salts were a combination of Epsom salts and geranium and juniper essential oils. Selena inhaled the scents of the oils and let them try to soothe her. They failed miserably, but she hoped the bath itself would do the trick.

Because the farmhouse sat at the front of their five acres, and the acreage was thick with apple trees around the back of the house, Selena never worried about pulling the shade over the window above the tub. Their property was secluded and private. No one was around.

Selena waited until the tub was half full. Then she

dropped her robe and started to pull off her nightshirt. When it was almost over her head, she froze. She yanked the nightshirt back down.

Someone was watching her. She was sure of it.

Selena leaned toward the window and scanned the backyard. She squinted and looked toward the trees. Her gaze shot from one tree to the next.

She didn't see anyone.

Selena frowned. Even more rattled now than she had been before, she reached out and pulled the shade. Then she turned and closed the bathroom door.

Selena's bath wasn't as relaxing as she'd hoped it would be. In fact, it was almost torturous. She tried several times to lean back and close her eyes, but she was too much on the alert. She kept thinking she could hear sounds coming from another part of the house. Once, she was sure she heard a creak in the attic overhead. Twice, she thought she heard footsteps on the stairs.

Finally, after just fifteen minutes, Selena gave up. She got out of the tub, drained it, and quickly put her robe on. Hurrying back to the bedroom, she dressed in jeans and a T-shirt. Then she went through the entire house, making sure she was alone.

Selena checked every room and every closet. She even looked inside the awful trunk, which was now back in the rear of the closet in the third bedroom. It was still empty.

After she assured herself that she was alone, Selena tried to work. It didn't do any good. She couldn't focus. She kept hearing sounds in the house. Once when the refrigerator's compressor kicked on, she practically leaped out of her chair.

Work wasn't working. She was a knot of nerves.

Selena abandoned her office. She grabbed her purse, went out to the pickup, and drove out of town. She spent the afternoon antiquing. Coming home with a vintage skirt, an antique hall table, and a pair of hundred-year-old pewter candleholders, she tried to tell herself she imagined everything that had happened the night before and that morning.

Over the next two weeks, though, it became abundantly clear that Selena hadn't imagined anything. She really was being watched. Either that or she was losing her mind.

No matter what Selena did when she was at home, she felt tingles between her shoulder blades. She could actually feel someone's—or something's—gaze boring into her. It wasn't just when she was alone, either. It happened when Cade was around, during the evenings and on the weekends, too.

After just a week of the unrelenting sensation of being observed constantly, Selena—lying awake during the night—decided that the cursory searches she'd done through the house . . . looking into every room and closet . . . weren't thorough enough. Selena's dad's wedding day advice burbled up and nudged at her: "Trust your instincts." Her instincts told her that she needed to look in every nook and cranny of her house.

When Cade left for work the next day, Selena made sure the house was locked up tight so nothing and no one could enter while she searched. Then she went through every tiny space in the house. She opened every cabinet and every drawer. She looked under every piece of furniture. She looked behind anything and everything that had more than an inch of space behind it.

In the middle of this search, though, in her bedroom, Selena stopped and sat down on the floor. She dropped her head into her hands. Who was she kidding? She wasn't being watched electronically. Not only was that totally unrealistic, it didn't fit the facts.

Selena got off the floor. She went down to her office and closed the door behind her. She pulled the shade. She sat at her desk and opened her laptop. She brought up a new document. At the top of it, she typed, "Facts."

Then she typed the facts as she knew them:

1. Lally was a robot that really existed.
2. Lally went missing from Freddy's Pizzaplex.
3. Cade saw Lally after it (*not "he," Selena refused to refer to Lally as "he"*) went missing.
4. Cade thought he trapped Lally in the trunk.
5. Cade kept the trunk with him, locked up, from that point on.
6. Selena unlocked the trunk.
7. When Cade opened the trunk, it was empty.
8. Selena saw Lally in the garage.

Selena had taken a symbolic logic class in college. It had been an elective, chosen as a lark, but what she learned came in handy now. She ran her facts through a logic equation and came up with two possible conclusions. Neither of them made her happy.

One logical conclusion, based on the facts, was that Lally was real. And although not as easily proven, the corollary to this conclusion was that Lally was watching Selena. This conclusion, however, was so insane (logical or not) that it led to the other possible conclusion: Selena was losing her mind.

Figuring they would help her in the business world, Selena had also taken several psychology courses in college. In one of the courses, they studied paranoia. Paranoid people, suffering from delusions, were always convinced their conclusions were logical. The problem, however, was that their conclusions were based on logical fallacies.

Selena went back over her list of facts. Was she really sure they were facts? Or was she just grasping at logic to cover up the real fact—that she was becoming paranoid and delusional?

Selena deleted the document and closed her laptop. Her hands were shaking.

She couldn't stay in this house another second.

Selena left her office. Ignoring the immediate awareness of being observed as she walked into the kitchen, she grabbed her purse and went out to the pickup. As she backed out of the garage, she realized where she needed to go.

"Well, hello, dear," Janice said when she opened her door and saw Selena standing on the front porch.

"I'm sorry I didn't call first, but—"

Janice waved away Selena's words. "What did I tell you about calling and about knocking on the door? My home is your home. You can come and go as you please."

Janice had given Selena a key to her house the day Selena and Cade married, and she had indeed told Selena to treat Janice's house as her own. Selena, however, hadn't been able to bring herself to do that. Besides, she was afraid that if she did so, Janice would assume the open-door policy was reciprocal. Selena loved Janice, but she didn't want her mother-in-law dropping in unannounced.

Janice, who was wearing a ruffled pastel-pink apron over yellow polyester pants and a yellow-and-green floral-patterned blouse, led Selena through the living room and into her large old-fashioned kitchen. Janice's leather flats tapped on the yellow-and-blue linoleum floor.

In the kitchen, Selena inhaled deeply. The room smelled like butter and cinnamon and sugar. The scent was enticing. It almost made her forget why she was here.

Janice gestured at the baking ingredients and pans scattered across her yellow Formica countertops. "I was just whipping up a batch of my raised cinnamon rolls for the ladies' club," Janice said. "Would you like to help?"

"I'd love to," Selena said honestly.

Maybe making cinnamon rolls was a better idea than having the conversation she wanted to have. Baking usually relaxed Selena. She hoped it would do so today.

Selena went into the pantry and plucked a simple blue apron (no ruffles) from the back of the pantry door. Janice had given the apron to Selena to use when they cooked together. "Frills just don't suit you, dear. You're far too beautiful to hide those elegant curves under flounces."

For the next hour, Selena and Janice spread out dough and sprinkled it with butter, cinnamon, and sugar. Then they'd rolled up the dough and cut it into classic cinnamon roll pinwheels. After the rolls were in the oven, Janice put water on for tea.

"Your usual peach spice, dear?"

"Do you have any chamomile?" Selena asked.

"Oh my," Janice said. "Do you need a de-stressor?"

"You could say that."

Janice didn't ask why Selena needed a de-stressor. Selena liked that about Janice—she never pried.

Janice made the tea, and she and Selena sat at Janice's round kitchen table. Selena toyed with a pale-blue-and-yellow plaid place mat as she let Janice chatter about her bridge club for a few minutes, but then Selena decided the conversation she came to have couldn't be put off any longer.

"Speaking of games," Selena said in what she knew was a pathetic segue, "what was it that Cade liked so much about Lally's Game?"

Janice didn't seem to mind the abrupt subject change. "Why, you know, I'm not sure." She took a sip of tea. "It's funny you ask. That's something I did wonder about at the time. At first, I thought it was the colors in the arena. He has never liked my softer color palette."

Selena thought about the rich burgundies, dark greens, and deep blues that Cade liked to wear with his ubiquitous khakis. She nodded.

"But I decided that wasn't right. I think what it

was"—Janice leaned back in her chair—"the game made him feel special. Because the game was just for two, and Lally was a robot, I think Cade felt like he was the chosen child or something. Now, heaven only knows why he needed that feeling. As an only child, he got nothing but tons of attention from me and his dad, until his dad passed, of course. Rest his soul." She shook her head. "But maybe that was part of it. He was an only child—maybe he wanted a brother. Maybe Lally was like a brother to him. I'm really not sure. I do know that Cade didn't want to share Lally with anyone."

"What do you mean?" Selena asked.

"Oh, I'm just remembering how upset Cade got one day when another little boy, a boy he knew from school named Daniel, snuck into the game. My oh my, was Cade angry. He was furious. His little face was all screwed up and red when he got home that day. 'The game is only for two!' he said to me over and over. You would have thought that Daniel had done something unforgivably egregious instead of just the relatively benign action of sneaking into Lally's Game with Cade." Janice sighed. "Daniel was a sweet little boy—adorable freckles across his nose. I knew his mother. It was so tragic that he died in a horrible accident."

Selena set down her teacup so fast it rattled in the saucer. Janice didn't notice. "What accident?" Selena asked.

Janice got up and walked over to the oven. She turned on the oven light and bent over to look through the glass window set in the oven door. "Oh, they're rising nicely. You're really getting the hang of kneading, dear."

"An accident?" Selena tried to get Janice back on track.

Janice acted like she didn't hear the question. Maybe she didn't. Selena had noticed that Janice tended to drift in and out of conversations at will, as if sometimes she had better things to think about than whatever was being talked about.

Selena tried a different question. "Why did Cade like Lally so much? I think Lally is kind of . . ."

"Scary-looking," Janice supplied.

Selena raised her eyebrows. "Yeah."

"I tend to agree," Janice said. "But then, little boys are odd creatures. Cade also liked snails and slugs when he was small. He was always poking at them with sticks—not to hurt them, mind you. He just wanted to see what they'd do. He thought they were fascinating."

Selena smiled at the image of Cade poking at a slug. Then her mind replaced the image of Cade and the slug with one of Lally. Selena shivered.

"How did Lally work, exactly?" Selena asked. "Was it programmed to run and hide, or to sneak up on the kids, or what?"

Selena wanted to understand how the robot could be doing what it was doing in her house. She was nearly 100 percent sure now that Lally was her stalker.

"Oh, no, nothing like that, dear," Janice said. "Lally didn't move. The kids had to carry him around and hide him themselves. Seemed somewhat silly to me. Of course if you hid the thing, you'd know where it was. But it was all a grand game of pretend, I guess."

Selena blinked at Janice. She opened her mouth to ask

another question, but no words came out. What else was there to ask? Selena knew what she needed to know.

Wiping her suddenly moist eyes with a trembling hand, Selena stood. "I have to get home and get some work done," she lied.

If Janice thought it odd that Selena practically ran out of the house and leaped into the pickup, Janice kept her reaction hidden. She smiled and waved as Selena drove away. Selena managed a twitchy wave in return. She couldn't summon up a smile.

Her hands gripping the steering wheel so tightly that they started to ache, Selena burned rubber as she accelerated away from Janice's home. She ignored the posted speed limit. Although her eyes were on the road, she wasn't really seeing it until her gaze flicked over an oncoming SUV. A very familiar SUV.

It was Cade.

Selena looked straight ahead as she passed her husband. Had he seen her?

Cade often got tunnel vision when he drove. Maybe he hadn't noticed the pickup. The bright red pickup.

Selena glanced in the rearview mirror. The SUV turned off, heading toward Janice's house.

So what if Cade did see her?

Maybe Selena was overreacting. Maybe she only thought she knew what was going on. And again, maybe she was leaping to logical conclusions that weren't logical at all.

A ripple of something that felt like static electricity

skittered down Selena's spine. Was it groundless anxiety, or was it thoroughly justified fear?

Selena didn't know. All she knew was that she wanted to get away.

Would she be fleeing from Lally . . . or from Cade? Or would she be fleeing from herself?

It didn't matter. She was fleeing.

Back in the farmhouse, Selena ran down the hall to the attic door. Hesitating for only a couple of seconds, she flung open the door and trotted up the steps. At the top of the stairs, she quickly pulled the string to turn on the bare bulb. She looked around. The attic looked the same as it had the last several times that she'd checked it.

Rushing across the open space, Selena grabbed two suitcases, the two largest. She pulled them across the attic. Their rubber wheels made scuffling noises against the buckled floorboards.

Selena shoved the suitcases out of the attic, onto the landing at the stop of the stairs. Then she dragged the cases down the stairs. The *skirr, thump, skirr, thump, skirr, thump* of their progress down the stairs made her cringe.

At the bottom of the stairs, Selena shoved the suitcases into the hall. She turned and closed the door behind her. She pulled the suitcases down the hall to the bedroom.

Selena hadn't allowed herself to sense anything since she'd left Janice's house. She didn't think she could function if she let herself feel.

When Selena lifted the suitcases onto the bed, though, her emotions demanded that she acknowledge them. She started crying.

"Stop it," Selena chastised herself. She wiped her eyes. She needed to focus.

Selena rushed to the bureau and began pulling out her clothes. She tried to think clearly enough to grab only what she really needed. Other than packing and getting out of the house, she had no clear plan in mind. How could she? She wasn't reasoning. She was reacting.

Selena finished with the bureau and started toward the closet. She was reaching for the door handle when she heard a thud downstairs. She froze.

Holding her breath, Selena listened.

She'd just started to breathe again when the *thud* was followed by a rustling sound . . . which wasn't far away. Selena turned and stared at the open bedroom door. Why hadn't she closed it?

Abandoning her packing job, Selena crossed to the open doorway. She looked down the hallway. It was empty.

A single tap came from the stairs leading down to the first floor. Selena glanced back into the bedroom. Should she ignore the sounds and just keep packing?

No. No way. If she wasn't here alone, she wanted to know about it.

Selena tiptoed toward the stairs. She craned her neck to examine the whole flight. It was empty. Selena looked around.

Okay, she'd do this systematically.

Starting with the empty bedroom, Selena began her search. She first opened the closet and checked the trunk. It was empty, of course.

Selena moved on to the bedroom they'd intended to turn into a spare room. It now had a bed, but the bed wasn't made up, and they hadn't added any other furniture. Selena got down on her knees and looked under the bed. Nothing.

She stood and went to the closet.

Selena had put the lesser-used part of her wardrobe in this closet. She had too many clothes . . . she knew that. But she loved clothes. She'd put most of her vintage finds in this closet.

Throwing open the closet door, she pushed back the long dresses and skirts. Nothing was behind them. The only thing on the floor of the closet was a couple dozen pairs of Selena's shoes—the ones that didn't fit in the master bedroom closet. On the shelf above the clothes, hat boxes containing the hats she rarely wore were stacked almost to the ceiling.

Selena left the guest room. She opened the linen closet. It, too, held only what it was supposed to hold: stacks of towels and sheets and bales of toilet paper and paper towels filled the closet's shelves. Selena closed the closet door.

Selena already knew nothing was in her bedroom. She'd just been in there. She'd also just checked the attic.

She had to go downstairs.

Selena walked slowly to the top of the staircase. She listened. Two clicks and a rattle came from the direction of the kitchen.

Selena steeled herself. She stepped as lightly as she could onto the first step.

Doing her best to avoid the creaky spots on the stairs, Selena crept down to the living room. There, she paused. A faint scratching sound came from the dining room. She headed that way.

They had yet to fill the hutch that had come with the cherry dining room set. Its upper display cabinets were empty. Selena hurried over to the hutch and opened its bottom cabinets. They were empty, too.

The dining room was separated from the kitchen by pocket doors. They were tucked back so the doorway was open. Selena stepped through it and surveyed the kitchen. It was deserted.

She crossed to the pantry. She opened the door and looked at the shelves full of canned and boxed foods and baking supplies and small kitchen appliances. She felt her tears trying to return. She'd had so much fun organizing the pantry. But that had been before . . .

A rasp came from the living room. It sounded like something was being dragged.

Selena grabbed a rolling pin from the nearest pantry shelf. She ran into the living room, the rolling pin cocked over her shoulder.

The living room was empty. Selena lowered the rolling pin.

Now what?

She'd searched the whole house.

She looked up the stairs, thinking about her abandoned packing job. Was she overreacting?

Selena walked over to the sofa and sat down. She

laid the rolling pin on the seat next to her. She leaned against the soft sofa back and picked up a taupe-and-cream-striped throw pillow. She hugged the pillow.

Was she just being paranoid? Was she about to blow up her marriage—her very new marriage—for no good reason?

Selena remembered her brother's wedding day advice: "Don't screw it up." *Was* she screwing it up?

Something rustled behind the sofa. Selena scrabbled for the rolling pin as she started to turn.

Before Selena could get a grip on the rolling pin or see what was behind her, a hand clamped over her mouth. Selena's heart kicked into overdrive. She tried to scream, but the hand stifled the noise.

Selena flailed for the rolling pin. The back of her hand knocked against it, and it rolled off the sofa. It hit the rug with a thunk.

"Shh," Cade said.

Selena twisted her neck so she could look up and behind her. Cade was leaning over the back of the sofa. Had he been hiding behind there?

Why?

What was he doing?

Had it been him making all those sounds?

Again, why?

Selena goggled at her husband.

Cade put his finger over his lips. His gaze, intense . . . almost deranged . . . darted all around the room.

Selena stared into the face of the man she'd loved for over two years. It was a face she thought she knew better than her own. And the man was someone she knew that well, too. She'd planned to spend her life with him; he was like an extension of her. Now she barely recognized him.

Yes, Cade still had the thick black hair and brows, the green eyes, the sculpted cheeks shadowed by his black whiskers as usual. He still had the wide mouth and the even white teeth. But all those features now looked distorted somehow. They looked like they'd been infected, tinged by something dark and menacing.

Selena tried to wrench her head away from Cade's hand. He pulled her tighter against the back of the sofa, turning her head so she couldn't see him anymore. She felt the pressure of his head against the top of hers.

"If you upset Lally," Cade whispered, "you'll end up in the trunk next."

Selena felt the bottom drop out of her stomach. She struggled to suck in air through her nose, which was partially covered by Cade's hot, hard palm.

Cade's breath was sour. He'd never had breath like that before. She'd smelled his morning breath and his garlic breath and his peanut butter breath, but this was acrid, as if he was exhaling whatever poison he'd kept hidden inside for many, many years.

"Promise you won't scream if I take my hand away," Cade whispered. His whisper was so quiet that Selena could barely make out the words. His warm, repulsive breath puffed into her ear.

Selena nodded several times. Why bother screaming? No one but Cade would hear her anyway.

"Promise?" Cade whispered.

Selena nodded again.

Cade took his hand away from Selena's mouth. She turned and opened her mouth. Cade made another shushing gesture. He leaned even closer to her.

"Don't speak. You *really* don't want to upset Lally," Cade whispered.

Selena used every ounce of willpower she had to keep her expression blank. She didn't move or make a sound.

Cade hurried around the sofa and sat down next to Selena. She didn't look at him again. She couldn't. She stared straight ahead. And she stayed silent.

Inside her mind, however, Selena was screaming her head off. She was tearing toward the door. She was coming to grips with the only logical conclusion presented by the facts: Her husband was insane.

Selena looked toward the entryway. Could she make it to the front door before Cade caught her?

She glanced at Cade. He cocked his head at her. Then he, too, looked toward the front door. He shook his head, slowly, once. He returned to scanning the room.

Cade was sitting close enough to Selena that she could feel the heat of his muscled thigh against hers. She was so familiar with the solid feel of him, but now the pressure against her own leg felt foreign, invasive.

"You killed Daniel, didn't you?" Selena whispered.

She didn't know she was going to ask the question until it was out of her mouth. She hadn't let herself consciously think about the conclusion she'd reached when Janice had told her about the boy who had died. But clearly, Selena had known. Why else had she raced home to pack? Why else had she planned to leave the man she loved?

Cade turned to stare at her. He shook his head. "No," he whispered. He shook his head again. "It was Lally." He turned and looked behind them. He craned his neck to look up the stairs. He shook his head a third time. "The game is only for two."

Prickles of terror cascaded through Selena's nervous system. Her throat closed, and she fought to breathe. Somehow, though, she was able to keep her expression tranquil.

Selena dropped her gaze, looking for the rolling pin. Her shoulders slumped. The rolling pin had spun over the rug when it hit; it was now under the coffee table. Selena would never be able to reach it before Cade reacted.

Turning toward Cade, Selena tried to look loving and concerned. "Knowing what Lally did must have been terrible for you," she whispered.

Cade looked at Selena as if he had no idea what she was talking about. She tamped down her revulsion and touched Cade's forearm. "Cade, honey, if Lally's in here, we need to leave. Why don't we leave?"

Cade frowned. He turned and looked toward the front door. He shook his head.

Selena didn't think. She just acted.

Leaping off the sofa, Selena lunged for the brass lamp on the nearest end table. She yanked its cord free of the plug set in the floor.

Cade started to stand and reach for Selena, but before he could, she gripped the lamp by its neck, crunching its drum shade. Then she swung the lamp like a baseball bat. She bashed its base against the side of Cade's head.

Cade staggered back, then fell into the coffee table. He hit his temple on the table, and he was limp when he slumped to the floor.

Selena didn't wait to see if Cade would move. She dropped the lamp and took off.

Because Cade's body blocked Selena's path to the front door, she started toward the kitchen. She hadn't taken two steps, though, when she saw a hint of white out of the corner of her eye. Selena whipped her gaze toward it. As she did, Cade moaned and shifted.

Selena lost her ability to reason. She turned and galloped up the stairs.

At the top of the stairs, Selena realized she'd been an idiot. She should have tried to make it to the back door. Now, though, she was on the second floor. Up here, she had no way out of the house unless she wanted to leap from a second-floor window. She glanced back down the stairs. She heard Cade groan again.

No, she couldn't risk going down there again. She looked down the hall. Where could she hide?

A scuffling sound came from the living room. Selena ran down the hall.

When she reached the guest bedroom door, she dashed into the room. She charged toward the closet, flung it open, and dove into the veil of her vintage clothes. She turned and pulled the closet door closed.

It might not have been the best hiding place in the world, but the familiarity of Selena's things gave her comfort. She could draw on that comfort to help her think about her next step. Right now, she didn't know what to do next. She knew she couldn't hide in here forever, of course. The house wasn't that big. If Cade searched for her, he'd eventually find her. Maybe before then, though, she'd come up with a plan.

Selena crouched behind the old dresses. Her breathing was so loud in the cramped darkness that it sounded like she was sharing the space with a pack of panting dogs.

Selena gulped air for several seconds. She had to quiet down. She couldn't listen for Cade if all she could hear were her own billowing inhalations.

Selena pulled herself into a tight little ball. She stared into the darkness pressing in around her. Although a trickle of light reached into the closet from under the door, it was only enough to give the clothes that shielded Selena a ghostly presence. Selena stared at the dim floating shapes and tried to steady her breathing.

Selena was starting to get control of herself when the clothing draped around her swished. And then a whisper came out of the darkness. The whisper's message was short, but it was filled with meaning.

"Hi."

Selena screamed louder than she'd ever screamed in her life.

Cade's consciousness swam in blackness. His thoughts were blanketed by the murk.

Through this mental nothingness, however, sound reached him. He heard the echo of piercing screams.

Then the curtain of oblivion muffled his hearing, too. He was aware of nothing at all.

Cade lifted his head. He groaned. It felt like a construction crew was pounding nails inside his skull.

Putting a hand to his head, Cade winced. He felt a knot near his temple.

Trying to sit up, Cade blinked to focus. The room spun. He was suddenly nauseous. He stopped moving and just sat, his back to the sofa.

Cade tried to find a coherent thought. His mind felt sluggish, mushy.

What was he doing on the floor?

Cade tried to remember . . .

Selena!

Cade struggled to his feet. The room spun again, but he managed to stay upright.

How long had he been out? He looked at his watch. Too long.

The fog in his brain cleared abruptly.

"Selena!" Cade called out.

Cade's chest constricted. He tore out of the living room.

Racing through the dining room, Cade burst into the kitchen. He sprinted toward the pantry and flung the door open. It was empty.

Barreling out of the kitchen, Cade hurried down the hall toward Selena's office. He looked into the room. When he didn't see her, he ran to the half bath. She wasn't there, either.

Cade returned to the living room. He checked the coat closet. He found nothing but coats and boots.

Cade pelted toward the stairs. He took the steps two at a time and was in the upstairs hallway in seconds. He rushed down the hall, throwing open doors as he went. He looked into the bathroom and his bedroom. He checked the master closet. Cade dashed back into the hallway. He started toward the guest room.

Then he stopped.

"No," he whispered.

Cade turned and looked toward the closed door of the third bedroom. The door was just a door, but it suddenly seemed to pulse in a rhythm that matched Cade's rapid heart rate.

Cade took a step toward the door. He wavered and steadied himself. He took another step.

Finally, he forced himself to move normally again. He ran to the door.

Cade's hand slipped off the knob when he tried to grasp it. His palms were sweating. He wiped them on his khakis and grabbed the knob again. He turned it.

Cade charged into the empty room. Not bothering to look around, Cade sped directly to the closet. Throwing the door open, he tossed aside the blankets piled on the trunk.

He dropped to his knees in front of it. Cade gripped the trunk's lid.

Taking a deep breath, Cade opened the trunk.

"No," Cade cried out.

Cade felt his face contort in horror. Tears filled his

eyes. He clapped a hand over his mouth so he couldn't be sick.

He wanted to look away from the grisly contents of the trunk, but he couldn't. As he continued to stare into the trunk, Cade's shoulders convulsed. His chest heaved.

Finally, he couldn't look any longer. He fell back. He dropped his head into his hands.

Cade's head whipped up, though, when a whisper came from above the trunk. It came from the empty shelf above the hanging rod in the closet. The whisper contained five familiar words:

"The game is only for two."

The hissed words drifted down to Cade like the spray of a toxic mist. They engulfed him, and then they left him in silence.

Cade reached the top of the staircase leading to the attic in his new house. He set down the stack of three boxes he'd lugged up the stairs. He looked across the attic at his beautiful fiancé. How could he have gotten so lucky? He'd hit the jackpot, again.

Debbie was gorgeous. Blonde, blue-eyed, petite, and as sweet as she was stunning—Debbie was any man's dream. And for Cade, she was a reality.

"Hey, babe," Debbie said. "This is the coolest, isn't it? I've never had an attic before."

Cade smiled. He loved Debbie's enthusiasm for life.

Above them, rain pattered on the attic roof. The gentle tapping was soothing. So was the dark, cloudy sky that hung low over the house like a gray shawl.

Cade and Debbie were moving into their new home, a big old Victorian on the outskirts of the city. They'd gotten the house for a song because it needed a lot of work. But Cade didn't mind; he liked a fixer-upper.

Cade walked over to Debbie and wrapped his arms around her slight shoulders. "Yes, it's the coolest . . . like you."

Debbie laughed. She tilted her head back and kissed the dimple on Cade's chin. Stepping out of his embrace, she looked around the room.

"I can't wait to finish this attic," Debbie said. "It will make an incredible art studio." She crossed to the big octagonal window at the east end of the attic. She threw her arms out and then spun in a circle. "When the sun's out, this window is going to let in some amazing light."

"An incredible art studio for an incredible artist," Cade said.

Debbie laughed. She returned to Cade. "You're the one who's incredible. Head programmer for the biggest tech company in the state. Hard to beat that."

Cade gave Debbie an "aw, shucks" look, but he didn't disagree. His new job was going to be great. He still couldn't believe he'd landed it. He couldn't wait to get started.

He'd had to move away from his mom to take the job, but she hadn't been upset about that. Janice had assured him she'd be fine.

"It was sweet of you to move back to be close to me, sweetie," she'd said, "and I loved having you nearby, but now . . . now I think you need to move on. And I'm perfectly capable of taking care of myself."

Debbie stepped away from Cade and started shifting boxes around. She set one box on top of a stack of two. Then she cocked her head and looked behind the stack.

"Hey, I've never seen this trunk before," Debbie said. "What's in this old thing?"

Cade crossed to Debbie and put his arm around her narrow waist. "Oh," he said, "it's just some childhood baggage."

Cade steered Debbie toward the attic door. "I'm ready for a break, babe. Aren't you? Let's go down and have some of that lemonade the new neighbor left for us. What was her name? Something old-fashioned."

Debbie smiled. "Winifred."

"That's it," Cade said.

Cade ushered Debbie out of the attic and turned back to flip off the light. Hesitating, half listening to Debbie chatter about an aunt who had the old-fashioned name of Octavia, Cade looked at the trunk. The battered old chest seemed to peer back at Cade as he gazed at it.

Cade turned off the light. He closed the attic door.

Thunder rumbled as the skies darkened even more. The attic was swathed in somber shadows.

Nothing but blackness could be seen in the vast space . . . until two small pinpoints of light peeked up over the top of the old trunk.

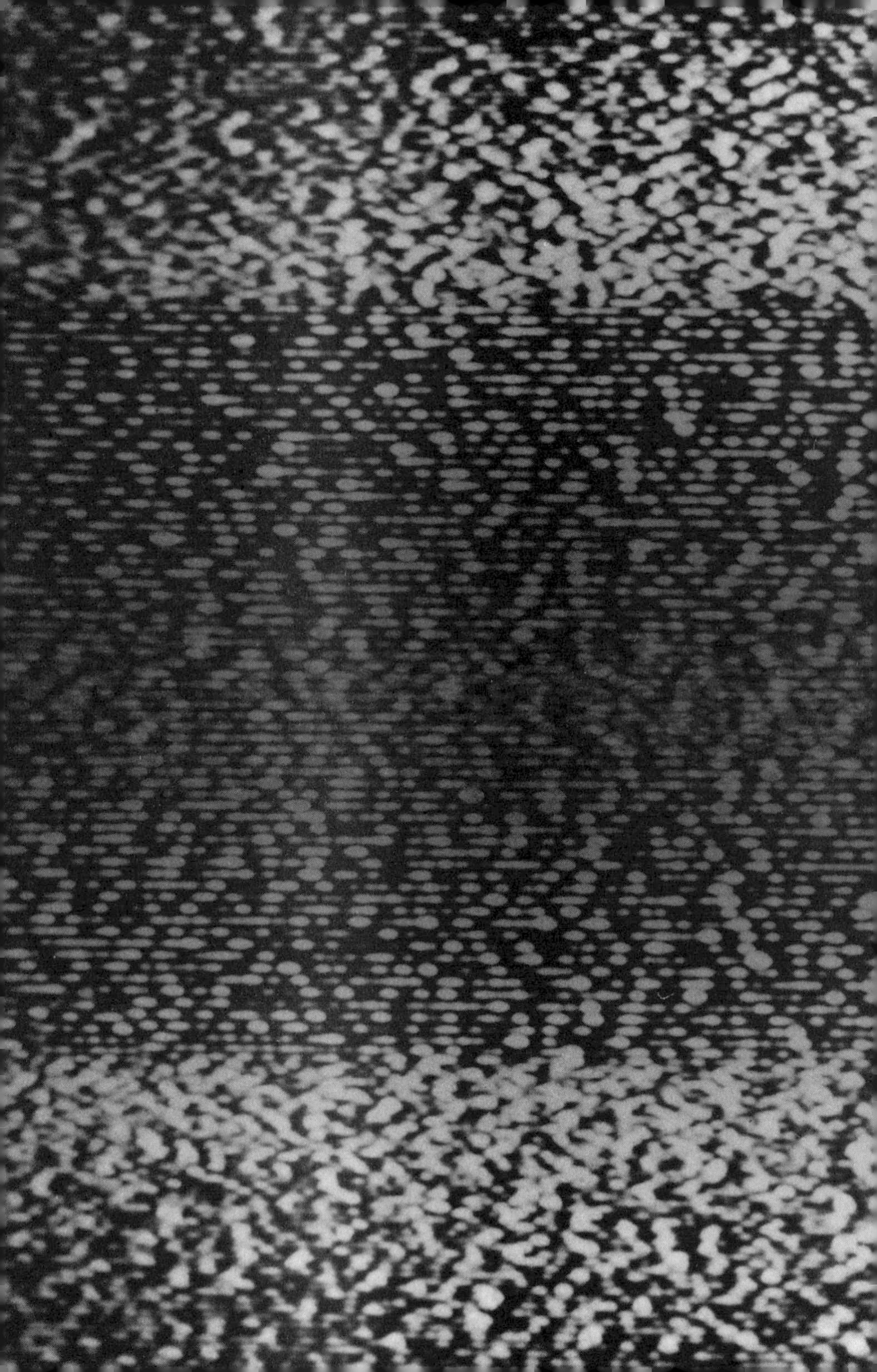

UNDER
CONSTRUCTION

"THIS IS UNREAL!" MAYA LOOKED UP AND CAUGHT HER REFLECTION IN THE NEON-BOUNDED, MIRROR-TILED CEILING. HER EYES GLOWED RED IN THE BLAZING LIGHT. FOR AN INSTANT, MAYA SHIVERED. THE WEIRD RADIANCE IN HER EYES MADE HER LOOK LIKE ONE OF THE UNDEAD FROM A ZOMBIE MOVIE. MAYA SHOOK HERSELF AND QUICKLY SHIFTED HER GAZE.

"Didn't I tell you?" Jaxon shouted to be heard above the blaring '80s rock music that pulsed around them. He brushed back his locs, took a huge bite of pizza, and looked from Maya to their strawberry-blonde friend Noelle, who was gazing in awe at the bright yellow roller-coaster track that wove in and out of luminescent climbing tubes entwined like snakes throughout the vast expanse beyond the dining area.

Noelle, her freckles standing out in the bright lights, reached for her soda. "I have to admit I thought 'Mega Pizzaplex' was more hype than reality, but this is pretty cool." She sucked through her straw and bopped to the music's beat. Her ponytail swung back and forth.

"Pretty cool?!" Jaxon dropped his half-eaten pizza slice. "This is *beyond* cool. I can't wait to try a VR booth."

"*AR* booth first, Jax," Maya said. She looked past a string of zipping go-carts and focused on the glass enclosure near the pizza-themed Tilt-A-Whirl (every pod on the ride was shaped like a pizza topping). The large, bubble-like booth was the whole reason she'd wanted to come here tonight.

Jaxon rolled his eyes. "Yeah, yeah, yeah, birthday girl. It's all about you." He flashed his signature mischievous grin and nudged Noelle, who gave Maya a goofy look.

Maya struck an exaggerated glam pose and checked herself in the overheard mirror again. In the psychedelic lights flashing around them, her long black hair looked like an oil slick reflecting a kaleidoscope. With her head tilted, her eyes no longer appeared red—they were their normal dark brown. She thought that between her dark skin and full features, her red dress, and the red rose tucked behind her ear, she looked a little like a flamenco

Maya returned her attention to her friends. She threw a balled-up napkin at them. "Just because I got to sixteen before you two losers is no reason to hate on me."

They all laughed.

Maya noticed that the bark of their laughter barely made a dent in the clamor around them. The music, loud as it was, competed with so many sounds that it was hard to distinguish them all. Maya could, however, make out the clatter of the roller coaster on its tracks, the hum of the go-carts, the tinny music and pings and bleeps of the arcade games, the buzzing sounds of laser tag, and, overlaying it all, the sounds of happy screams and shouts and chatter. Maya's sister, Elena, would hate this place, Maya thought affectionately. Elena liked things quiet and peaceful. Freddy Fazbear's Mega Pizzaplex was the exact opposite of quiet and peaceful.

Elena would have hated the bright-colored chaos in the Pizzaplex, too. Whereas Maya loved vibrant jewel tones, her sister was all about white and gray and pastels. Maya looked down at her bloodred dress, then shifted her gaze to Jaxon's bright orange shirt and Noelle's hot pink blouse. She glanced around. Even their bright clothes were lost in the rainbow-scape of the Pizzaplex.

Maya and her friends were squeezed into a corner booth in the main dining area. The room was huge, but it was so stuffed with shiny-red-laminate-topped tables and chrome-backed chairs that it seemed smaller than it was—especially because every table was filled with voracious families, kids, and teens chowing down on pizza. Servers clad in red Freddy Fazbear uniform shirts, with multicolored glow necklaces looped around their necks, could barely squeeze through the aisles as they rushed through the room serving pizzas and drinks. The swinging doors to the kitchen on the far side of the room were in almost-constant motion.

Everywhere Maya looked, brilliant color and sparkling light beamed and blinked and shimmered. It seemed like everything in the Pizzaplex was spectacularly illuminated. LED lights were everywhere. They formed frames around all the tabletops and the flashy Freddy-themed posters on the walls, and outlined the squares of the black-and-white-checkerboard floor. Anything not wrapped and highlighted in LEDs was brightened by neon. Glowing archways formed the entrance to the dining area and to every other entertainment venue in the Pizzaplex. Alternating with the LED-wrapped Freddy-themed posters, neon art in the shape of Freddy's characters and pizza wedges blazed bright in reds, blues, greens, yellows, pinks, purples, and oranges. The mirrored ceiling caught all this light and refracted it, sending prisms of color everywhere. Outside the dining area, in the center of the Pizzaplex's domed roof, a backlit pizza-motif, stained-glass cupola in the center of the round mall's ceiling beamed streams of even more color down over the constant movement below. Maya thought that the effect was like a ballet of every tint she'd ever seen—the whole place seemed to flare and flicker in a constant motion of dazzling bright hues.

"You know sixteen is just a construct, right?" Jaxon shouted.

Maya flinched when a speck of partially chewed pizza landed on her arm. She wrinkled her nose and brushed it off. She was used to Jaxon spitting food across the table. He got so excited when he talked. When he got revved up about something, his words would run together and he'd forget to breathe. At the end of his all-too-frequent monologues, he'd be gasping for air.

"A person's age isn't real," Jaxon continued. "It's just a thought. Its existence depends on the subject's mind."

Noelle groaned. "Oh, not again. Can't we leave science in science class?"

Maya patted Noelle's arm in sympathy. However, the truth was Maya liked science—even when she didn't always understand it. Maya's main interest was biology, specifically botany. She loved growing things—her mom said she was a born nurturer. But Jaxon's musings about physics could be fun to listen to.

Noelle frowned at Jaxon. "And besides, age isn't a thought. It's an empirical fact. Maya has been alive for sixteen years, no matter what her mind has to say about it."

Jaxon waved as if swatting away Noelle's words. Maya stared at Jaxon's big, dark hand. Jaxon was tall and ebony-skinned. His mother was Jamaican, and his dad was from the deep South. He looked like he should be a star basketball player, but he hated sports. He was all about science and philosophy. He loved to ask unanswerable questions and try to answer them for hours on end.

"But what's *alive*?" Jaxon countered Noelle's logic. He leaned forward, practically bouncing in his seat. "Last night, I read an article about something called 'quantum immortality.' It's a theory that says we never actually die."

Noelle looked up at the mirrored ceiling as if it could help her. She sighed so loudly that not even the cacophony around them could silence her exasperation.

Jaxon ignored her. "See, it's related to the many-worlds theory. No matter which branch of reality you follow, your consciousness is experiencing existence. Each path leads to more existence. We can never experience anything but existence. So, we go on and on."

"Well, *you* sure go on and on," Noelle said.

Maya laughed.

Noelle didn't even smile at her own joke. She crossed her arms and gave Jaxon a hard look. "People die all the time. The idea of immortality is totally wack! Are you telling me that when my uncle died, he didn't really die?" Her voice rose at the end of the question.

Noelle had been very close to her uncle, and she'd been shocked and devastated a couple weeks before when he'd been killed in a car accident. Maya briefly touched Noelle's arm gently.

Jaxon, as typically oblivious to real emotion as usual, didn't notice Noelle's upset. "Well, quantum immortality only applies to the observer. So, we actually can't know for sure if he's really dead. I mean, his consciousness could have branched onto a path that hasn't led to his death. No one has seen what the endgame would look like because the observer hasn't been there yet. What seems real to us may not be what's actually real, so . . ."

Maya, noticing Noelle's darkening expression, poked Jaxon. "Are you done eating yet? I want to head over to the AR unit."

Jaxon glanced at his empty plate. He looked surprised to find it pizza-less.

Noelle exhaled as if blowing out her upset. She cocked her head and pointed at Jaxon. "Pizza is a construct, you know," Noelle said. "It only exists in your mind."

Jaxon grinned. "Touché, girl." He offered Noelle his fist, and she, having apparently forgiven him his insensitivity, bumped his fist with hers before she stood.

Maya, Jaxon, and Noelle linked arms as they left a VR booth and stepped into the throngs rushing from one entertainment venue to the next. Noelle squealed when she bumped into an employee wearing a Montgomery Gator costume. The phosphorescent-green gator mascot patted Noelle on the head and moved on.

"Roxanne Wolf is a great character," Jaxon gushed. "Did you see . . . ?"

Maya tugged on his arm. "Yeah, we saw. Hey, I let you drag me into a VR booth, and now it's my turn. Come on. The AR booth is this way."

Jaxon resisted her. He pointed at a line twisting toward the entrance to the roller coaster. "I want to go on Fast Freddy," Jaxon said. "It's supposed to have all the latest in roller-coaster high tech." Jaxon pulled a brochure from his pocket. "It says here that each car has a touch pad, and you can pick your own music. Five genres to choose from. There are 28 LED lights programmed to change color throughout the ride." Jaxon pointed past the long lines. "And see? It has a moving loading platform. It never comes to a complete stop." He waved the brochure. "And it has cameras, some on board and some on the track. Lasers trigger timing devices and computers record the images and create a video that's synced to whatever music you pick. The video is downloaded and sent to that kiosk." Jaxon pointed at a small hut-like structure that was covered in strobing lights. "It's all done in under a minute so you can get the ultimate souvenir to go. Now that would be a great birthday present, don't you think, Maya?" Jaxon inhaled deeply to refill his lungs.

Roller-coaster cars careened past overhead. Maya felt a rush of air brush against her face. The screams of the coaster's riders hurt her ears. She shook her head. "Later. AR booth first."

Jaxon hung his head. Then he bowed elaborately. "Whatever thou dost sayest, milady."

Maya laughed. Jaxon's Southern accent destroyed his attempt at Old English. "Come on," she urged her friends.

Noelle and Jaxon followed Maya's lead. She tugged them away from the roller-coaster entrance and on past the giant swings and bumper cars.

At first, Maya hadn't been that into the idea of celebrating her birthday at Freddy's Pizzaplex. When Jaxon had shown her the advertisements for the place, she'd thought they were so over-the-top that they were lame. She had to admit that Fazbear Entertainment knew how to make money. Before the Pizzaplex's big opening, the company sold thousands of mini hologram projectors at super-discounted prices, and the first thing the projector displayed was a holographic Glamrock Freddy doing his spiel:

"Hey, kids! Do you want pizza?! Well, Fazbear Entertainment has spared no expense developing the world's most extreme family fun center—Freddy Fazbear's Mega Pizzaplex! At three stories tall, it's the flashiest, raddest, rockingest, safest pizzeria the universe has ever seen. Of course Freddy and the band are excited to meet you! Utilizing the latest in animatronic technology, you can actually party with the stars themselves. So, on your next birthday, let Freddy Fazbear's Mega Pizzaplex make you a SUPERSTAR!"

"It's the perfect place to celebrate your sweet sixteen," Jaxon had said.

Maya had resisted Jaxon's pitch even when he'd listed all the entertainment possibilities. "Of course they have a stage for the animatronics' performances, and they have an arcade and laser tag," he'd told her, "but they also have a theater, giant swings and slides and climbing tubes, and rides—including a dope roller coaster and bumper cars and state-of-the-art, electric-powered go-carts and a sweet carrousel. Oh, and carnival games. Maybe I can win you a plush Freddy."

"Be still, my beating heart," Maya had replied.

When Maya had kept shaking her head, Jaxon had talked even faster. "They also have sick VR booths and Role Play venues. Oh, and they have this AR unit especially for birthdays. It's their premier attraction, because

Freddy's has always put an emphasis on celebrating birthdays."

"I know what VR is, but what's *AR*?" Maya had asked despite herself.

Jaxon's eyes had lit up. He loved explaining things. "AR stands for augmented reality. It's a way of crossing the real world with the virtual world. Basically, objects in the real world are enhanced by computer-generated perceptions. The one at the Pizzaplex is supposed to be a really awesome one; it uses all sorts of sensory modalities—visual, auditory, somatosensory, olfactory, and even haptic."

"Haptic?" Maya had questioned.

"Haptic means to grab on to something . . . basically, the AR unit at the Pizzaplex lets you reach out and grasp things that aren't even really there. AR basically plays with reality. The tech can be both constructive and destructive, meaning that it can add things into the physical world or subtract things. Whereas VR completely replaces reality with a simulated one, AR is a mix of the real and the virtual. The AR unit at the Pizzaplex is called 'The World Celebrates You!' It gives you the illusion that everyone in the Pizzaplex is taking part in celebrating *you*. Basically, it's like having a massive birthday shindig without all the money and the trouble. It's the ultimate way to spend a birthday!"

This was what convinced Maya to go for Jaxon's idea. Even though she knew her family and all her friends would celebrate her birthday, she also knew it wasn't going to be a huge deal. Her family didn't have the money for a "shindig" like she wanted. It sounded pretty neat to have a whole Pizzaplex full of people partying with Maya on her birthday. So here they were, and she wanted to get her party started!

Maya and her friends had been at the Pizzaplex for a few hours already. They'd wandered at first, then they'd eaten (at Jaxon's insistence), and then they'd gone to the VR area (again, at Jaxon's insistence). During this time, Maya had gotten a pretty good sense of the place.

The Pizzaplex was set up in a circle. In the center of the circle, ramps led down to a blacklight enclosure created for the littlest kids. The cave-like area was filled with glowing climbing bars, slides, and foam building blocks; all this was set up around a glitter-ball pit. Padded benches for watchful parents surrounded the area.

Above this subterranean play area, a grandiose two-story theater rotunda erupted like a fairy-tale castle under the stained-glass cupola. The rest of the entertainment venues and shops (of course stores in the Pizzaplex carried Freddy's-themed clothing, costumes, souvenirs, and toys) ringed the Pizzaplex. Between these venues and the theater, a go-cart track crisscrossed over and under the walkways that led from one part of the Pizzaplex to the other. Several VR booths were spaced along the walkways. And above everything, the roller-coaster tracks intertwined with the climbing tubes. The two systems looked like a serpentine modern art installation, or a hovering serpent waiting to devour all the people bustling about beneath it.

Maya dragged her friends through the crowd, yanking

on Jaxon as he tried to veer toward the Role Play area. Her gaze was set on the prize: the AR unit. It was only a few yards away and it was . . .

"Closed?!" Maya exclaimed.

Maya stopped so abruptly that Jaxon ran into her. Noelle plowed into Jaxon. The two grunted and glared at Maya. Then they looked in the direction of her gaze.

The AR unit looked like a giant snow globe . . . only without the snow. Its base was bright red, and inside the clear, thick glass, a throne-like gold upholstered chair sat in the center of the clear bubble. A flashing neon sign blinked above the spherical glass: THE WORLD CELEBRATES YOU! Neon stars and streamers surrounded the words.

Unfortunately, another sign was attached to bright yellow tape—similar to crime scene tape—stretching across the entrance to the AR unit. That sign read: CLOSED. UNDER CONSTRUCTION.

"Under construction?!" Maya snapped. "How can they make a big deal about a 'premier' attraction and not even finish it before they open? That's false advertising!"

Maya turned to scowl at Jaxon. "You said I'd get my big party!"

Jaxon's usually animated expression was slack as he looked at the closed AR unit. His shoulders slumped. "I'm sorry, Maya. I didn't know."

Noelle hugged Maya. "Come on. It's not that big a deal, is it? You've got us. And"—she swept her arm outward to indicate all the commotion in the Pizzaplex—"it's not like there's nothing to do."

Maya blinked away tears that had come out of nowhere.

She felt like a spoiled brat for being so upset, and she didn't want to cry in front of her friends. But she was so disappointed. She'd really looked forward to using the AR.

Maya glowered at the closed sign. Then she set her jaw and took a deep breath. She looked around. No one was paying any attention to her and her friends. She made up her mind. She rushed forward and ducked under the yellow tape.

Noelle gasped. "Maya! You can't go in there!"

Maya stepped over the threshold and looked back at Noelle and Jaxon. "Looks like I can. Are you coming?"

Noelle shook her head. She glanced over her shoulder and looked up. Maya followed Noelle's gaze.

A huge mirrored, curved enclosure loomed above a large area marked EMPLOYEES ONLY—the space looked big enough to house all the behind-the-scenes offices and machinery that must have gone into operating something as elaborate as the Pizzaplex. It was clear the mirrors were two-way, and the elevated enclosure was where security kept an eye on the Pizzaplex. Obviously aided by the dozens of CCTV cameras Maya had noticed everywhere she and her friends had been, Maya was sure a bunch of self-important, low-paid employees were playing Big Brother up there. Yeah, they could be watching, but she didn't care.

"They can come and drag me out if they want," Maya said. "I'm going in. Come with me, or don't."

Noelle and Jaxon exchanged a look. Jaxon shrugged. "What's the worst they can do? Throw us out?" He looked longingly at the roller coaster, then shrugged again. "We can always go home and work on our science projects."

Noelle blew a raspberry. "As if."

Maya turned her back on her friends and entered the AR booth. She only got a few feet into it before she heard Jaxon and Noelle rush in behind her.

"This is cool!" Jaxon circled the chair, then bent over and examined it. "There's a processor under here." He gestured at the glass that surrounded them. "The glass will be the display that adds to what you can see through the dome now." He reached down and picked up a woven-looking headband that had been lying—almost hidden—on the chair's seat. "This looks like a sensory device. See?" He held up the headband and indicated a latticework of nodes on the inside of it. "I think this will augment your senses to make your experience feel real in every way. I think the way it works is—"

"Whatever," Maya said. She darted to the chair and grabbed the headband. If security had seen them enter the AR booth, she didn't have much time. She took a seat.

Maya slipped on the headband. She looked around. Nothing had changed. "How do you turn it on?" Maya asked.

Jaxon bent down. He fiddled with something.

Suddenly, the glass walls of the AR booth disappeared. Maya could see directly out to the huge expanse of the Pizzaplex. And it was filled with birthday balloons, streamers, and piles and piles of birthday presents. It was also filled with hundreds of people blowing noisemakers and cheering. It was as if everyone in the Pizzaplex had stopped to focus on Maya!

All the adults and kids on the walkways were turned to look at her. All the people in the dining room were gazing her way, their glasses raised. The rides were still in motion, but all the people on them were craning their necks to see Maya as they zipped past or spun around. Patrons and employees alike were smiling toward Maya as if she was the most important person on the planet.

"Surprise!" they all shouted in unison.

Maya felt a thrill of importance as she gazed out at the crowd. Then she teared up again when she spotted her family. They were all there. Her parents and Elena, her aunt Sofia and uncle Rafael. Her aunt Luciana and uncle Peter. She saw all her cousins, even her favorite—little Axel. She saw her neighbors: The Davis twins were jumping up and down and waving at Maya, and the Thompsons' three kids held a big HAPPY BIRTHDAY banner. Even old Mr. and Mrs. Lambert—the grumpy couple who lived across the street from Maya's home—were in the crowd. Mrs. Lambert held up a plate of her award-winning coffee cake ("grand prize winner at the county fair for twenty years straight, dear"); Maya's love of that coffee cake was what had endeared her to the otherwise curmudgeonly couple. Maya saw her favorite teacher, Mrs. Carpenter, and her minister, Pastor Ben. She saw all the members of her choir and her classmates from school. Everyone was wearing party hats, and everyone looked like Maya's birthday was the happiest day of their lives.

As Maya strained to try to pick out all the people she knew, the crowd parted, and Glamrock Chica—her bright pink dress shining under the bright lights—skipped into view, heading toward Maya. She pushed a big cart. The cart held a massive, six-tiered birthday cake frosted in creamy icing and decorated with red candy roses—Maya's favorite flower. Sixteen huge candles flickered atop the cake.

Maya realized she was smiling so widely that her cheeks were starting to hurt. But she smiled even wider when Freddy's band started a boisterous rock version of "Happy Birthday," and everyone started singing along.

Maya reached out and grabbed Jaxon's and Noelle's hands. "See? It wasn't offline after all."

"Happy Birthday, Maya!" Noelle hugged Maya, then stepped back so Jaxon could follow suit.

Maya smiled at the cherry scent of Noelle's shampoo and the smell of Jaxon's pizza breath. She understood that the scene in front of her wasn't real. The Pizzaplex couldn't have suddenly transformed into the birthday party of her dreams. All the people she knew didn't just beam in magically, and the ones she didn't know of course weren't interrupting their fun to make such a big deal of a total stranger. But it *felt* real. And the familiar smells of her friends anchored her to what was *really* real.

The combination of real and not real was heady. It spun Maya out of herself and into the fantasy of frolic and laughter.

At first, it felt like Maya was just watching the celebration around her, but as it continued, she was no longer an observer. She was drawn into the party just as she would have been if it was real.

After Freddy's band finished the Happy Birthday, everyone started chanting. "Make a wish! Make a wish!" Maya grinned and imagined having this moment last forever. Then she blew out the candles. Their smoke spiraled upward as everyone cheered. Maya laughed in delight.

Freddy's band started playing one of Maya's favorite rock songs. Jaxon grabbed Maya's hand, and he spun her into the crowd, which backed up and formed a circle around a makeshift dance floor in the center of the walkway.

Jaxon and Maya weren't a couple—she thought of him as more of a brother than a friend, but the two of them had always danced well together. Jaxon had some serious moves, and Maya was naturally graceful. As they started popping to the staccato beat of the song, they slid into a series of intricate steps that they'd never practiced but had to have looked choreographed to their audience. Maya felt like a dancing queen as Jaxon whirled her and dipped her and even flipped her over his shoulder.

When the song ended, the crowd went wild, and more couples filled the open space as a new song began. They danced and danced and danced.

Maya didn't know how much time had passed when Jaxon, sweaty and grinning like a maniac, led her through the crowd to the cake. There, Glamrock Chica handed Maya a gleaming knife—which might have looked scary in any other setting—and Maya cut into the second tier of her gorgeous cake. She got the first piece, and she nearly fainted in bliss when her teeth sank into the moist pistachio-and-buttercream-flavored confection. Her favorite flavors.

Several employees rushed out to help hand out cake. They all hugged or high-fived Maya as they passed her. She didn't know any of them, but they all acted like they had been longtime friends.

The music was still blasting, and the crowd was still laughing and dancing and chattering. Maya felt a little like a bouncing beach ball as she was passed from one group of revelers to the next. She was hugged over and over and over. She received kisses and pats and "love you!"s from all her relatives. Her favorite kiss was from sweet little Axel—the lip smack was wet and sticky from the smear of frosting on his mouth.

Time continued to expand and compress in an odd and disorienting way as Maya suddenly found herself seated near the massive pile of brightly wrapped presents. Her mom, after whispering that Maya's special present from her grandparents would come later as usual, began handing Maya the presents, and she opened them one by one.

Most of the presents were wrapped in floral-themed paper; everyone knew how much she loved flowers. All the gifts inside the festive packages were things she loved; she received vibrantly colored clothes, stacks of romance novels and books on gardening, sheet music and CDs of her favorite music, makeup and jewelry, stuffed teddy bears, posters and prints of flowers and cute kittens, scented lotions and soaps and candles, a portable keyboard, a new guitar, and, finally, a new laptop and a camera (these were to help her photograph and catalog the flowers she grew, her mom said). The gift opening seemed endless. Maya actually started feeling guilty; she was sure that watching her open presents had to be boring for everyone else. Whenever she looked up at the people surrounding her, though, they appeared to be enjoying themselves; they were totally attentive.

Maya couldn't imagine a more perfect birthday celebration. She wanted it to last forever.

Maya, Jaxon, and Noelle ducked under the tape and looked out at the boisterous groups of kids and families enjoying the Pizzaplex. "I can't believe this looked like my birthday party a few seconds ago," Maya said.

"I told you it would be great." Jaxon beamed as if he'd designed the AR unit himself.

Maya leaned into him. "Yes, you did. And you were right!"

"*I* can't believe we didn't get thrown out of there," Noelle said, looking up at the security booth.

Maya followed Noelle's gaze. She frowned. Noelle had a point. Surely, they had cameras in the AR unit; someone must have seen them.

Maya shrugged. "Whatever. I'm just glad I got my big party."

"Now can we go on the roller coaster?" Jaxon asked.

Maya laughed. "Yes. Let's go on the roller coaster."

The friends linked arms again, and they headed for the roller-coaster line. As they made their way through the crush of happy people, Maya felt like she was more floating than walking. Her virtual—or augmented or whatever—birthday party was the best birthday celebration she'd ever had. It wasn't that she didn't appreciate the birthday picnics her family usually organized for her—the pot-luck affairs that were always held in their yard and always included a basic sheet cake and a cheap piñata. But she'd wanted the kind of party she'd just had in the AR unit. Now she'd had one. She was a happy girl.

"I admit that this coaster is flashy-looking," Noelle said as they queued up for the ride, "but I don't see how a three-story roller coaster can be much fun. It won't get high enough." She gazed up at the roller coaster's apex.

"It's not the height that makes it thrilling," Jaxon said. "It's the speed, and the loop-the-loops, and the . . . other things."

"What other things?" Maya asked.

"You'll see," Jaxon said in ominous tones. "Mwah ha ha ha."

Noelle rolled her eyes. "It can't be that scary."

But it was.

Maya and her friends didn't have to wait long before they were the next ones in line for one of the yellow-and-red-striped cars coming toward the continually moving loading area. The cars were big enough for three people if they didn't mind a tight fit, so Maya and Noelle followed Jaxon into one of the cars. They pulled the safety bars tightly over their chests as instructed, and as soon as the bars clicked into place, the car disappeared into a dark tunnel.

"Rock and roll, right?" Jaxon shouted as he reached

for the touch pad in front of them. The pad was the only thing lit up in the blackness.

"Always!" Noelle yelled.

Throbbing base notes ushered in a screeching guitar riff, and the car picked up speed. As it accelerated into a turn, a giant pirate fox suddenly loomed in front of them. Raising a gleaming hook, the fox swiped the sharp steel at their heads just as the car jerked to the left.

Maya and Noelle screamed. Jaxon whooped.

The car swung around in a tight loop, then shot upward and flipped over, whipping them—upside down—into another U-turn before suddenly flipping them back over and climbing.

From that point on, the ride was a blur for Maya. Every few seconds, it seemed like another Freddy's character—lit up blindingly and larger than life—appeared out of nowhere and scared them silly. After the third jump scare of sharp animatronic teeth speeding toward her face, Maya closed her eyes. From that point, the ride was a mayhem of motion and sound and light flashing behind her eyelids. Thankfully, it was over seemingly as fast as it started.

When the car slowed, the safety bars released and Jaxon jumped out of the car. Noelle clambered after him. Maya brought up the rear, staggering. She was sure the ride had stolen some of her bones; her legs felt like jellyfish tentacles.

"Wasn't that the boss?!" Jaxon shouted as he grabbed Maya's and Noelle's hands. "Let's go get our videos." He pulled them toward the little kiosk near the coaster's exit area.

A couple minutes later, they had their custom videos. Maya wasn't sure she'd ever look at hers. She didn't need to watch a closed-eyed version of herself being terrified at a hundred miles per hour, or however fast they'd been going. Jaxon had kept yelling out the speeds during the ride, but Maya had ignored him.

"Now what?" Jaxon asked.

Maya shook her head. "Your choice, Jax." She'd come here tonight for the AR birthday party, and she'd gotten that. She didn't really care what they did now.

It was after ten when Maya pushed open the back door to her family's small, bright kitchen. She hung her keys on a peg by the turquoise retro fridge.

Her parents, as she'd expected them to be, were sitting at the multicolored-tile-topped table, sipping hot chocolate and playing a game of cards. It was their sometimes pre-bedtime routine, and Maya suspected it was a good excuse for them to wait up for their teenage daughter to get home.

Maya's mom drew a card and smiled up at Maya. "Have fun, sweetie?"

Maya grinned. "It was great! Even better than Jaxon said it would be. You won't believe everything they have there. The . . ." Maya stopped. She'd been about to tell them about the AR unit, but to do that, she'd have to tell them about the dream party with everything she'd ever wanted in a birthday party. She didn't want them to think she didn't appreciate the parties they had for her.

"Did you go on the roller coaster?" Maya's dad asked. "I read about it. I bet it's pretty cool."

Maya laughed. "You sound like Jaxon. He couldn't stop talking about it." Maya held out the videotape she got at the kiosk. "Here's a video of our ride. You can see me screaming and closing my eyes as tight as I could get them closed."

Maya's mother shook her head. "Oh, *that* sounds like fun." Her words were dripping in sarcasm.

Maya went to her mom and gave her a hug. Laying her cheek against the top of her mom's head, she closed her eyes to soak in the smooth softness of her mom's short black curls, peppered with gray. Her mom smelled like jasmine, as always.

Maya straightened, then stepped around the table and bent over to give her dad a quick hug. The top of his head wasn't soft. He kept his thinning hair in a buzz cut, which felt like a big burr against Maya's chin. But she didn't care. She loved her dad, and the way he always smelled like ink and toner.

Maya let go of her dad and turned to the gas stove—like the fridge, it, too, was turquoise and styled to look like a holdover from the '50s. She knew there'd be enough hot chocolate for her left in the pan. She poured it into a mug and joined her parents at the table.

She took a sip of the rich chocolate. "Deal me in next round?"

"Absolutely," her dad said.

Maya smiled as she watched her parents finish out their hand. For the thousandth time, she thought about how lucky she was to have such great parents. Her mom—dark and petite and pretty—was a grade school teacher, but she always had plenty of time to take care of her family. Maya's dad, his plain face creased with smile lines around his eyes and mouth, ran an office supply and print shop. He worked long hours, but he somehow always made Maya and Elena feel like they were the center of his world. He spent time with them every day.

As her parents finished their hand, and her dad dealt out the cards for a new hand, Maya thought again about the AR unit party. She wasn't sure why it had been so important to have that experience of being the focus of everyone's attention; it wasn't like she was neglected. Maybe it was that her parents were so laid-back that nothing ever felt like a huge deal. Sometimes Maya wanted things to be exciting instead of just happy.

Maya picked up her cards. For now, though, breathing in the aroma of the chocolate in the mug in front of her and gazing at her parents' content faces, she was okay with happy.

After a half hour or so of cards, Maya kissed her parents, said good night, and headed down the narrow hallway to the bathroom. She took her time in the hall, pausing to gaze at the dozens of framed family photographs that covered the walls. Of course the photos had been there for years, but the party had reminded Maya of all the people who loved her. She wanted to linger over their images for a few seconds before brushing her teeth.

When Maya finally got to her room, she didn't even bother to change into pajamas. She was suddenly wiped out. She just fell back onto her twin bed. She hit the mattress with such a big *whomp* that the bedframe scooted along the wood floor.

Elena sat up in the other twin bed stuffed into the small room. "Whah?" In the muted yellow glow of a domed nightlight, Maya could see Elena's face was crumpled, and her curly black hair was in a tangle.

"Sorry, El," Maya said. "It's just me."

"Time is it?" Elena rubbed her big brown eyes, ones that looked just like Maya's.

"Late." Maya hopped off her bed and moved to Elena's bed. "Scoot over."

Elena grumbled, but she scooted. Maya cuddled in next to her sister and wrapped her in a hug. Maya savored the soft warmth of her sister's flannel-clad shoulders as she looked around their small bedroom.

Containing just the two beds and one nightstand, along with one dresser and a table that served as a desk for both of them, the room had been Maya and Elena's domain for their whole lives. Maya remembered when the room had been painted pink and the bedspreads had been white and frilly. Now half the room was painted Maya's favorite color, red, and half the room was painted gray. Maya's bedspread had a rose design. Elena's was pale blue.

Maya thought about all the presents she'd received at her big birthday party. She smiled. It was a good thing they hadn't been real. How would she have fit all that stuff into this tiny room? Too bad the AR couldn't have conjured up a big house for her and her family.

But that was just silly. Maya loved this compact house.

It was filled with happy memories. How could a new, big house compete with that?

"What's going on?" Elena asked.

Maya laughed. "It's my birthday, that's what."

Elena squinted at the glowing blue numbers on their clock radio, which sat on their shared nightstand. "Not for another forty-two minutes and fifteen seconds."

Maya laughed again and squeezed her precise sister. "Close enough. Besides, I already had my big party."

Elena frowned. "But I wasn't there."

"Yes, you were! Everyone was. It was the best party ever!"

Elena wrinkled her broad nose and made a face at Maya. She wriggled free of Maya's embrace. "You're weird."

"*You're* weird."

Elena rolled her eyes and flopped back onto the bed. "Get out of my bed. I need my brain sleep."

Maya smiled. Maya's mother was always telling her girls they needed their beauty sleep, but cerebral and not-concerned-with-beauty Elena took issue with that. She said she got brain sleep that helped her be smarter.

Whereas Maya had gotten looks, Elena had gotten brains. Elena might have been shorter and plainer than Maya, but what she lacked in beauty she made up for in smarts and confidence. Elena was a year behind Maya in age; she was years ahead of Maya in education and accomplishments. Maya was content to be a teenager. Elena was in a hurry to be an adult. She was a math whiz, and the following year, she was going to be enrolled in the local college. Maya wasn't envious at all about Elena's brilliance. In fact, Maya was super proud of Elena. Maya was content to be Maya, and she celebrated Elena's Elena-ness. It had been, however, incredibly nice to be the center of attention at her Pizzaplex birthday party. Maya didn't usually get to shine like that. It was an experience she was never going to forget.

The next day, Maya's family threw her the usual birthday party on the porch and grass in front of their house. Because the home's front yard was small, the party always spilled into the street and into the neighboring yards. Even though decorations were minimal, the giant oaks and weeping willows that sheltered the small houses in the neighborhood provided all the beauty Maya could have asked for. Maya's birthday was in May (apparently inspiration for her name), and it was always warm out this time of year. As usual, iridescent hummingbirds and fluttering yellow monarch butterflies were flitting around in the flower beds at the base of the porch rails in front of Maya's house. They were better than balloons.

This year, besides the customary simple HAPPY BIRTHDAY banner strung across the front of the house, the decor also included a SWEET SIXTEEN sign Maya's youngest cousins had made. The big cardboard sign was lettered with crayons and decorated with glitter and childlike drawings of red roses. The piñata was the usual vaguely shaped horse form (Maya didn't even like horses), and the cake was a big flat chocolate one with a slanted "Happy Birthday, Maya" written in store-bought tubed icing.

The celebration couldn't have been more different than the one at the Pizzaplex. The only similarity was the presence of all Maya's family and friends and Mrs. Lambert's offering of her award-winning coffee cake. The cake was actually welcome; Maya preferred the apple-and-crumb-topped cake to the chocolate one her family always had for her.

"Thanks for coming, Mr. and Mrs. Lambert," Maya said when she went to sit with them. They had brought their own folding chairs and had set themselves up under the gnarly oak near the street. They watched the party as if it was a war instead of a celebration—deep frowns etched between their brows.

"Hmmph," Mr. Lambert said predictably.

"I hope you enjoyed my award-winning coffee cake," Mrs. Lambert said.

"It was delicious, as always!" Maya told her. She wanted to hug the old lady, but Mrs. Lambert's erect posture and stiff shoulders were as good as a KEEP AWAY sign.

Maya left the Lamberts and headed back toward the porch. As she crossed the yard, she rubbed her temples. This morning, when she'd gotten up, her forehead had hurt—right where a couple of the AR headband nodes had touched her skin. She'd figured the headband had just irritated her skin, but the pain felt more like a mild headache now.

"Hey, birthday girl!" Noelle called out.

Maya forgot about her headache and joined her friends.

After the birthday cake had been cut, Maya and the other kids and teens took turns swatting the piñata. As always, the Davis twins—towheaded Wesley and Wendy—swinging in unison, were the ones who cracked the papier-mâché open. Then they fought each other for first grab at the candy. Everyone else hung back. The tall and gangly thirteen-year-olds' competitions were infamous—it was best not to get in their way.

Although this party did have a small table of gifts, the present opening wasn't a focal point of the affair. Maya's mom always emphasized that gifts were optional. "*Presence* is much more important than *presents*," her invitations always said. She knew the people in Maya's neighborhood and at her school weren't well-off.

The custom at Maya's family's parties was for the birthday celebrant to open a present here and there, if the person giving the gift wanted to see it opened. As usual, the most eager of Maya's gift givers were the Thompson kids.

Donny (ten), Parker (six), and Aurora (five) were Maya's three favorite kids (after her cousins, of course). She was their frequent babysitter because their parents, still pretty young because they'd married when they were eighteen and had Donny a few months later, hadn't yet grown out of their need to party. They went clubbing regularly. They were great parents, though, and Mrs. Thompson was an awesome baker. Maya loved lingering in the Thompsons' pristine kitchen after the couple got back from their dates. "Snickerdoodle time!" Mr. Thompson would say, and Maya and the Thompsons would each eat one of the big, soft cookies while Mr. Thompson told jokes. His favorite jokes were typical dad humor.

"Knock, knock," Mr. Thompson had said a few nights before.

Maya had answered dutifully, "Who's there?"

"Alpaca."

"Alpaca who?"

"I'll packa the luggage. You'll packa the car."

Maya and Mrs. Thompson had groaned in unison.

Mr. Thompson always managed to make Maya laugh several times as he walked her home. The cookies and the jokes were great, but the couple paid Maya well, too.

For the last three years—since they'd moved in a few houses down from Maya's home—the Thompson kids had made Maya birthday presents. The first year, they gave her bookmarks made from tongue depressors (Mrs. Thompson was a nurse) and crayon-and-glitter-decorated brown lunch bags that looked like they'd already been used. Last year, she'd gotten a "necklace" made out of pipe cleaners. This year, the kids had gone all out; they'd made her a scrapbook constructed from more brown lunch bags and filled with glued-on buttons, string, and photos of the three kids.

"This is wonderful!" Maya gushed when they insisted she open their present.

"I picked out the buttons!" pug-nosed Aurora announced. She beamed with pride, and her brothers snorted.

"Well, you did a great job. I appreciate all the effort you put into it," Maya told them. The kids accepted her thank-you hugs and scampered off to see if Wesley and Wendy had left any candy behind.

Maya appreciated everything about her party, and she had a great time playing with her cousins, especially little Axel, Aunt Sofia and Uncle Peter's youngest. Axel was a pudgy-faced four-year-old with dark, dark eyes, and a grin that never disappeared. Maya loved babysitting him. He was obsessed with patty-cake, and they played it so long that Maya's palms were sore when Axel finally got drowsy enough to curl up in her lap and go to sleep.

When Aunt Sofia, her long braids looped on top of her head in an intricate knot, picked up her youngest son, she kissed Maya on the forehead. "*Feliz cumpleaños, mi sobrina.*"

"Thanks, Aunt Sofia." Maya grinned when Sofia raised an eyebrow. "I mean *gracias, Tia Sofia.*"

Maya's grandparents had come to the US before they had their children, Sofia, Luciana, and Maya's mother, Violeta. They'd learned English right away, and they made sure their three girls were bilingual from the start. The same was true of their grandchildren. Between them, Maya's mother and aunts had given Maya's maternal grandparents twelve grandchildren. Sofia and Peter were responsible for six of those. Luciana and Rafael had four kids. Maya's mother brought up the rear with her two girls. Recently, Sofia had become obsessed with celebrating the family's Puerto Rican heritage, and she was taking Spanish lessons. She was insistent that Maya learn, too. Maya humored her with the occasional phrase.

Thankfully, Maya's dad's parents weren't as interested

in their ancestors' roots. "Mostly, we're Irish, but I think we have some Czech, some Greek, and some Welsh in us," Maya's father had told her when she'd asked about it. She was glad no one was obsessed with that heritage; she couldn't even imagine trying to learn Gaelic or even more difficult, Czechoslovakian. She was also glad that her father was an only child. Not that she didn't love her cousins—she did. But family get-togethers were chaotic enough without even more little kids running around.

After Maya's aunts and uncles and cousins left, Maya and her parents settled in with Maya's grandparents around a small bonfire in the backyard. It was the family's tradition that the grandparents gave their grandchild a special birthday present after the party was over. Maya always loved this part of her birthday, just as she loved her grandparents.

Maya's two sets of grandparents couldn't have been more different. Her mother's parents were dark-skinned, short, and round, their faces lined from years of smiling, their hands calloused from years of working. They ran a construction business. In their early sixties, they could both wield a hammer as well as any of their younger employees—even Maya's gran could drive a nail in with just two strokes. Maya's father's parents, on the other hand, were tall, pale, and soft-looking. Self-professed aging hippies, "Nana" and "Pappy" were artists, and the only thing their hands revealed were the colors of the paint they were using in their latest creations. They looked younger than their sixty-some years, and they sounded even younger than that.

"So, you're sixteen, Maya," Pappy said now. "Right on." He patted her knee.

Maya noticed that age spots were joining the freckles on the back of Pappy's hands. Pappy reflected the Irish part of her dad's family background. Whereas her dad had black hair, Pappy's hair was deep auburn.

"Because this is a special year, sweetie," Nana said, "we all chipped in together to get you something, well, special." She looked at her husband and at Gran and Gramps. "Isn't that right?"

Gran nodded. She pulled a small red velvet pouch from the pocket of her gingham apron, which she hadn't removed even though she'd left the kitchen hours before. She held it out, and Maya took it.

Maya pulled at the pouch's string, and she turned the pouch over. A thin gold chain with a delicate gold rose pendant fell from the pouch.

"Oh," Maya gasped. "It's beautiful!"

Nana elbowed Pappy. "I told you she'd love it."

Pappy shrugged. He winked at Maya. "I voted for one of those video game contraptions. I thought someone your age would want something more techy."

Maya shook her head. "I've had techy already, Pappy." She smiled widely as she thought about her virtual birthday party from the night before. "This is perfect."

Elena helped Maya put the necklace on, then hugged her sister. "Happy Birthday, big sis."

Maya's parents and grandparents hugged Maya in turn. When they were done, Maya's dad, firelight making the scalp showing through his thinning buzz cut appear to shine, got out his guitar. Maya and her parents and grandparents sang old folk songs for the next hour, until Elena said her brain needed its sleep.

When Maya settled under the covers that night, listening to Elena's snores (her sister always fell asleep in seconds), Maya pressed her fingers to her forehead. The slight headache that had nagged at her off and on all day was throbbing more insistently now. Was the pain related to her time in the AR booth? *No*, Maya thought, *it was probably just a coincidence*. She was simply overtired.

Maya closed her eyes. It really had been a perfect birthday. She'd had her big party and her traditional party. All was well in her world. Maya closed her eyes and relaxed into sleep.

When Maya looked back toward the end of everything, she couldn't easily pinpoint when it all started to go weirdly wrong. She remembered the first shock, of course. But at the time, it didn't seem all that strange. Sad, yes, But not strange. After all, it wasn't unusual for sixty-two-year-old women to get breast cancer. And it wasn't unusual for them to lose their battle with the disease, even after weeks of chemotherapy and radiation.

Besides Gran's cancer diagnosis, nothing out of the ordinary happened in the year following Maya's sixteenth birthday. Things were pretty normal . . . except for Maya's recurring headaches. The headaches, though annoying, had never been serious enough for her to tell anyone about them. Secretly, she'd wondered if the AR booth's headband had done some kind of nerve damage.

However, since the booth had been closed when she'd used it, she didn't think she had any right to complain to anyone about it. Besides, the pain was low-grade and intermittent. She told herself it was nothing.

Maya's seventeenth birthday was nothing like her sixteenth. Although Gran tried to insist that the party go on as usual, no one was in the mood to celebrate anything. By the night before Maya's birthday, Gran was like a transparent copy of her old self, as if someone with shaky hands had tried to transfer her likeness onto flimsy tracing paper.

On the night of Maya's seventeenth birthday, Maya wasn't sitting around a bonfire with her parents, sister, and grandparents. Instead, she and Gramps, Maya's parents, her sister, her aunts and uncles, and her cousins clustered around Gran's bed in Gran and Gramp's living room. Gran had insisted on passing away at home, so they'd turned the previously cozy and comfy room into a sickroom. It was a room barely large enough to contain all of the people who'd come to say good-bye to the wasted woman in the narrow bed. And it was a room not nearly big enough to contain all the love the family had for this woman who was close to taking her last breath. The room also was inadequate to hold the grief that was born and grew to its full stature the second Gran was gone.

Later, as Maya and Elena clung to each other in Elena's bed, Maya asked, "Why Gran? Why not mean old Mr. Vance from down the street? I saw him kick his dog once. He's a jerk. Why not him?"

Elena hugged Maya tighter. "It doesn't work like that.

There isn't some good and bad list like Santa has. It's biology and chemistry and DNA and . . ."

"And BS. It's BS, Elena. It's just . . ." Maya burst into tears. She touched the gold rose that hung from her neck. She hadn't taken off the special necklace since she'd put it on. She held it tight now, as if by holding on to it she could hold on to her gran.

When Maya finally crawled into her own bed and tried to settle in to sleep later that night, she wasn't relaxed at all. All was not well in her world. She'd just lost one of her favorite people on the planet. What would be next?

The answer to Maya's question came within just a few days. Pappy was diagnosed with cancer next; it was in his brain. And it was fast growing. He was unable to care for himself within a month of getting his diagnosis. Maya and her extended family took turns doing everything for Pappy. And before Pappy reached the end, Gramps got his diagnosis.

"He's not going to fight it," Maya's mother said to Maya's dad the day they got the news. Maya and her parents were at the dinner table, picking at plates of spaghetti. No one had an appetite. Maya's mother, though, was stoic; her eyes were dry. Maya, on the other hand, felt like she was drowning in tears. She had trouble breathing, too; it was as if a big troll had settled on her chest and was squeezing the air out of her. Why was this happening to her family?

As Maya got ready for bed that night, Elena sat in front of the computer they shared. "If it was just Gran and Gramps," Elena said, tapping a few keys, "I'd suspect something carcinogenic in their building supplies. But it's Pappy, too. Maybe his paints?"

Maya looked over her sister's shoulder. As Elena clicked the mouse, the display shifted from an article to the words "Page Under Construction." Elena sighed dramatically.

"I'm going to bed," Maya said.

Elena said, "Mm," and clicked the mouse to open a new search window.

For the next several nights, Elena stayed up late, researching the causes of cancer. Maya wasn't good at research, so she spent her spare time reading to her grandfathers. Pappy, of course, didn't understand her anymore. But she knew he was aware of her presence. Gramps kept telling her she should stop wasting her time catering to a dying "old fart." "You should be out on a date," he told her several times.

Maya tried to remember the last time she'd cared about going on a date. Just a few months before, she'd had a crush on the junior varsity quarterback. Now when she looked at his carefree grin and his tousled hair, she just felt annoyed.

Wrapped up as she was with her sick grandparents, Maya didn't pay any attention to what was going on with anyone else. It was only after Nana got cancer and died, just days after Gramps and Pappy were gone, that Maya emerged from her grief fog enough to notice that people all around her were getting the dreaded disease.

Mr. and Mrs. Lambert succumbed not long after Maya's grandparents passed. Maya hadn't even known they'd been sick until their grown children showed up to close up and sell the house. Maya felt bad when she found out; she hadn't been over to see them since Gran had gotten sick. Weirdly, she vaguely wondered what would become of Mrs. Lambert's award-winning coffee cake recipe.

But she didn't think about that for long.

Mr. and Mrs. Davis were diagnosed next. Then Mr. and Mrs. Thompson. Maya hadn't even noticed she hadn't been asked to babysit for a while because she'd been so preoccupied with her grandparents. When she found out they were sick, she went to see the Thompsons, and she offered to help take care of them and the kids. She did the same for the Davis family. Running back and forth between the two homes and her own took up all her free time after school.

At school, she was barely conscious. However, she was aware enough to notice that she was hearing the word *cancer* far more than she should have been.

"My brother was admitted to the oncology ward last night," Brynn, the varsity head cheerleader, said to her crew as Maya shuffled past their table in the noisy cafeteria.

"We're taking care of my sister at home," Brynn's best friend, Makenzie, said. "The hospital said the oncology ward is full. Actually, there aren't any beds in the whole hospital. When people go to the ER, they park the beds in the hallway."

Brynn had no response to that. The other girls at the table were equally unconcerned.

Maya stopped and stared at them. They didn't notice her.

"Did you try that new mascara I told you about?" Brynn asked one of the other girls.

The girl, a pretty blonde, fluttered her eyelashes. "Can't you tell?"

Everyone at the table admired the girl's long lashes. Maya shook her head and took her tray over to the table where Jaxon and Noelle were already seated.

Maya flopped into a plastic chair and slammed her tray on the scarred laminate-topped table. She gestured toward the cheerleaders' table. "Can you believe them? They're acting like it's no big deal."

"Like what's no big deal?" Noelle asked.

Maya frowned at her friend. "All the cancer."

Jaxon shrugged. "My mom was diagnosed last week."

Maya's mouth dropped open. "I'm so sorry! You didn't say anything!"

"What's to say?" Jaxon asked. He dug into the chili on his tray. The pungent scents of tomato and onion filled the air. "Y'all want to go to the Pizzaplex this weekend? Apparently, the new animatronics show is pretty incredible."

Maya stared at Jaxon. She shifted her gaze to Noelle, who was nibbling at a salad. Noelle was totally relaxed.

"Seriously?" Maya said. The word came out high-pitched and too loud.

Jaxon and Noelle frowned at Maya. Several kids at neighboring tables turned and looked at Maya with raised eyebrows.

Maya lowered her voice and leaned toward her friends. "Why are you acting like everything's normal?"

Jaxon and Noelle exchanged a baffled look. Jaxon gazed across the table at Maya. "Um, because everything *is* normal?"

Maya slapped her hand on the table. The *thwack* cut through the chaotic conversations and the tinkling cutlery sounds in the room. For a second, the sounds stopped, and several heads rotated Maya's way. Maya ignored the scrutiny.

She kept her voice low and steady when she spoke again. "Haven't you noticed that it seems like everyone's getting cancer? My aunt Sofia was just diagnosed. My uncle Rafael was diagnosed a month ago. And my grandparents have all died of it in the last thirteen months. It's weird. Something's going on."

Jaxon shrugged. "Cancer sucks, for sure. But there's nothing weird about it."

Maya opened her mouth to argue, but what was the point? She picked up her tray and stomped out of the cafeteria. She no longer wanted to hang around with her friends. They were clueless. She couldn't stand looking at their carefree faces.

Over the next few weeks, Maya saw less and less of Jaxon and Noelle. Summer arrived, and her friends got jobs at the local burger joint. Maya didn't have time for a job. She split her time between the hospital, where she'd sit with her aunts and uncles (Aunt Lucia and Uncle Peter had cancer now, too) while they received chemo, and her aunts' and uncles' houses, where she would help take care of the older cousins, four of whom were now dying of cancer. She also still helped out the Davises and the Thompsons.

Maya spent her days making food, changing sheets, emptying bedpans, and doling out medications. She spent her nights tossing and turning and listening to Elena snore.

When Maya's grandparents had gotten sick, Elena had been a compatriot in Maya's need for answers. But Elena had long since stopped going to the library. When Maya would ask her why so many people were dying of cancer, Elena would just shrug and stick her nose back in her latest math textbook.

Maya sometimes thought of trying to figure out what was going on herself. Although she didn't like doing research, she knew how. But when did she have the time? She was too busy taking care of sick people.

One afternoon in late August, just days from the start of Maya's senior year, Maya finally got a bit of good news. Her favorite teacher, Mrs. Carpenter, had her first baby. Noelle stopped by to tell Maya about it.

The two girls stood in front of the washer and dryer in Maya's house. Maya's father had been sick for a month. Because her mom was focused on caring for him, Maya was now doing everything else in the house—the cooking, the cleaning, the shopping, the laundry, even paying the bills. She wasn't sure how much longer she'd be able to do that. Her dad's chemo treatment was making him really weak. How long would he be able to keep working?

"How'd you hear?" Maya asked as she and Noelle folded a sheet.

"My mom is in the hospice ward at the hospital. When I get bored sitting with her, I go to the nursery to look at the babies."

Maya wanted to call Noelle out on the offhand way she talked about her mother's condition, but she also wanted more to focus on something hopeful for a change. A new baby was hopeful.

"Is she still in the hospital?" Maya asked. "Mrs. Carpenter, that is?"

Noelle shook her head. "I think she and the baby went home." Noelle's eyes lit up. "Do you want to go see them?"

Maya nodded. "She doesn't live too far from here. Let's ride our bikes."

It took only fifteen minutes for Maya and Noelle to pedal the few blocks to Mrs. Carpenter's house. They reached the small cottage-style home just as a summer storm cloud released a downpour and thunder rumbled across the sky. They dropped their bikes in the narrow driveway and scurried to the covered front porch.

When they knocked, lightning lit up the sky behind them. Thunder sounded again just seconds later as Mrs. Carpenter opened her door.

"Girls! What a nice surprise!"

Mrs. Carpenter wasn't a whole lot older than Maya and Noelle. She'd started teaching in Maya's sophomore year. She was a tall, slender woman with wavy brown hair and bright green eyes; she could easily have passed for a teenager, even now, standing in her entryway holding a blanketed bundle to her shoulder.

Maya craned her neck to get a glimpse of the child. "Congratulations!" Maya said. "We came to see your baby." Maya held out a bunch of roses she'd picked from her backyard right before she and Noelle had hopped on their bikes. With everything that was going on, Maya hadn't had time to tend her flowers, but they seemed to be taking care of themselves. The peach-colored blooms in Maya's hand were healthy and fragrant.

As she held out the flowers, it suddenly occurred to Maya that they should have brought something for the baby. "Oh, I'm sorry," Maya blurted. "We should have brought a toy or something for her. Her? Or him?"

Mrs. Carpenter backed up and motioned for the girls to come into her house. They stepped into a cramped but tidy living room. It was bright, with white walls and yellow-upholstered furniture. The room smelled like lemon furniture polish. And the whole house smelled like fresh-brewed coffee. This surprised Maya; she'd been in her aunts' and uncles' homes after each of her younger cousins had been born. Their houses had always smelled like a mixture of dirty diapers and talc and spit-up and sweet milk—it was what Maya thought of as "baby smell," a distinctive scent that seemed to come with infants.

"Her," Mrs. Carpenter said. "I've named her Cecilia." She stopped in front of a small stone fireplace. "Would you like to hold her?"

"Sure!" Maya accepted the bundle Mrs. Carpenter offered her.

Pulling the baby close to her chest, Maya inhaled and

smelled . . . nothing. She took another sniff. Nope. Not a single thing. That was weird.

Maya shifted the baby, carefully cradling the baby's head with one hand. With the other hand, Maya pushed back the blanket that swathed the infant's face.

Maya gasped.

And she almost dropped Mrs. Carpenter's baby.

Mrs. Carpenter's *baby*?

Maya gazed in horror at the thing she was holding. It was all she could do not to thrust it back at Mrs. Carpenter and run screaming from the house.

Swallowing hard, aware of sweat trickling down her spine, Maya looked up at Mrs. Carpenter. Mrs. Carpenter beamed at Maya, then looked with pride and joy at her new daughter.

Maya shifted her gaze to Noelle. Had Noelle seen what Maya was holding?

Yes. Noelle was looking right at the baby's face.

But really, there was no face to look at. There was a head, yes. But the head was featureless. It looked like an unfinished, see-through doll's head.

Struggling to keep her expression composed, Maya started rocking back and forth as if she was holding a real baby. With a quavering voice, she began singing a lullaby.

Noelle started talking to Mrs. Carpenter about feeding schedules, and Maya turned away from her friend and her teacher. She surreptitiously peeled back the blanket so she could see the whole of the . . . thing . . . in her arms.

No, this wasn't a baby. She didn't know what it was. But it wasn't a baby.

Smooth and limp, like a jelly-filled, lifeless rag doll, the floppy content of the baby blanket was an inert mannequin-baby contained in a revolting slick, translucent skin. Beneath the skin, the very faintest outlines of pale blue filaments extended throughout the thing's body. They looked like veins, sort of. Other than these barely perceptible strands, the thing's filling was as clear as its outer covering.

The summer before Maya and her friends had visited the Pizzaplex for her AR birthday celebration, Jaxon had dragged Noelle and Maya to a sci-fi movie about cloning. The thing Maya held reminded her of the unfinished clones. It wasn't an infant. It was like a placeholder for an infant.

"Shall I take her?" Mrs. Carpenter said.

Maya whirled around. She tried to find her voice, but she couldn't. She silently nodded and returned the flaccid . . . what? . . . being? Creature? Not baby, that was for sure.

Maya handed Cecilia to her mother.

"Can I get you girls a snack?" Mrs. Carpenter asked.

"No thank you," Maya said just as Noelle said, "Sure."

Mrs. Carpenter looked from Maya to Noelle. Maya frowned at her friend.

"I need to get back home," Maya told Mrs. Carpenter. "I have a lot to do."

"It was sweet of you to visit," Mrs. Carpenter said. "Cecilia likes being the center of attention." Mrs. Carpenter looked down at Cecilia as if the baby was the cutest thing in the world. "Don't you, little one?" Mrs. Carpenter nuzzled the baby's smooth, flat squishy face.

Maya felt nauseous. "Um, we need to go. Bye, Mrs. Carpenter."

Maya grabbed Noelle's hand and pulled her friend out of the teacher's house.

In the driveway outside, Maya sucked in air that smelled of ozone and damp earth. The thunderstorm had left as quickly as it had arrived. The ground was soaked, and the sun's warmth was turning the wetness into steam that drifted up from the dirt and pavement like ephemeral ghosts. Maya leaned over and held her stomach. She felt dizzy and weak.

"Are you okay?" Noelle asked.

Maya straightened. She shot Noelle a baffled look. "Didn't you see that?"

"See what? Cecilia? She's a cute baby." Noelle studied Maya. "What's wrong with you?"

Maya didn't have time to think much more about Mrs. Carpenter's "baby" the rest of that day. Well, that wasn't true. Even though she was busy, Maya really couldn't think of anything *but* Mrs. Carpenter's baby, and Noelle's weird reaction to "her." But it creeped Maya out so much, she forced herself to focus on something else every time the image of the droopy, dollish infant-thing entered her mind.

By the end of the day, she'd convinced herself she'd imagined the whole thing. Besides, the news she got over dinner shoved aside everything else: her mom now had cancer.

They gave Maya this news calmly as Maya's mom dished up beef stew, and her dad handed around the bread basket, a basket that contained rolls that reminded Maya of Cecilia's featureless head.

Nope. *Stop it*, she told herself. She was *not* going to think about that.

Maya handed the basket to Elena without taking a roll.

Maya wasn't hungry anyway. She picked up her spoon and swirled it in her stew, making circular patterns in the tarragon-scented broth. Her parents were going to die. How could they sit here eating as if everything was okay? Why was Elena chattering about her upcoming college classes?

Maya dropped her spoon with a clatter. "Elena, stop it!" she snapped.

Elena froze with a baby head—no, bread roll—halfway to her mouth. She lifted her eyebrows. "What's your problem?" she asked Maya.

"How are you going to be able to go to school if Mom and Dad are gone?" Maya asked. She looked from Elena to her parents.

Maya's dad patted Maya's hand. "Oh, don't worry, sweetie. You and Elena will be fine. I know it seems like we don't have much, but we've been saving. There's plenty of funds to get you both through school. And this house is paid for."

Maya's dad returned to peacefully eating his stew as if he'd just been discussing the day's thunderstorm. "This is wonderful, hon," he said to Maya's mom. "As usual."

Maya's mom smiled. She picked up the bread basket and offered it to Maya. "Are you sure you don't want a roll, sweetie?"

Maya erupted from her chair, covered her mouth, and

ran from the room. She barely made it to the bathroom before she threw up.

Did she have cancer now, too?

No, Maya didn't have cancer. Her mom took her to the hospital the next day. Doctors ran the usual tests. Maya, unlike most of the world's population now, was fine.

Although *fine* wasn't the right word to describe Maya at all. There was nothing fine about her. Maya was a wreck.

Although school had started again, it wasn't the way Maya had envisioned her senior year. For one thing, most of the regular teachers were dead or dying. Half her class was sick.

Maya's favorite activity, choir, was canceled, as were most extracurricular activities. There weren't enough participants.

And even so—no one acted as if anything was wrong.

Maya had never liked watching the news. No one in her family did. They preferred talking about happy events and doing fun things than keeping up with what was going wrong in the world. But lately, Maya couldn't *stop* watching the news. She found herself glued to the TV screen whenever she was within range of one. It was like watching a car wreck. It was horrifying, but she couldn't help herself.

The news mesmerized her not because it was all doom and gloom, though. In fact, the news was the exact opposite of the panic that would be reasonable in the current situation. Instead of sober reports of illness and death, the newscasts provided sprightly updates on the number of people diagnosed, being treated, and dying. It was like watching a ticker tape of cancer stats, all scrolling across the screen to a backdrop of upbeat instrumental music and the newscasters' chirpy narration.

"Another 342,128 people died in China yesterday, Bob," a poofy-haired female news anchor announced as if giving a football score. "How are things in Europe?"

"Similar, Pam. The last count was 312,572," Bob responded. "Britain has passed a mass-cremation law to handle the large numbers of deceased."

As freaky as these emotionless reports were, though, they weren't what kept Maya awake at night. Her eyes weren't glued open in the darkness because of the cancer. Not even her own sick family kept her awake. No. What kept her from closing her eyes were the babies. Or really, the *not*-babies. She couldn't stop thinking about the unfinished, vaguely baby-shaped things that were now passing for newborns in the world.

Mrs. Carpenter's Cecilia was the first one that Maya saw, but now she knew that Cecilia wasn't an aberration. All new infants looked like Cecilia. None of the babies were normal.

And worse than that. Not only were they not born normal, but these new children also weren't growing normally, either.

A couple days after seeing Cecilia for the first time, Maya had gone to the pharmacy. Skirting around a SIDEWALK UNDER CONSTRUCTION sign, Maya had spotted

Mrs. Carpenter getting into her car. "Hi, Mrs. Carpenter," Maya had called.

"Hi, Maya!"

"How's Cecilia?" Maya had asked, just to be polite. She didn't really want to know anything about the thing Mrs. Carpenter called her baby.

"Oh, she's great," Mrs. Carpenter had said, and she'd gestured toward the passenger seat of her SUV.

Looking past Mrs. Carpenter, Maya had glanced at the bundle she'd expected to see strapped into a baby carrier. But what she saw on the passenger seat wasn't a baby-sized bundle. It was a *child*-sized . . . what? Mass?

So unstructured that it was little more than a vaguely human-shaped outline, the thing that Mrs. Carpenter called Cecilia was a *drooping* pile of gooey material spilling over the edges of the passenger seat. Unmoving, the child-thing drooped across the leather lifelessly. But it wasn't lifeless. How could it be? It had more than quadrupled in size in just two days!

And Mrs. Carpenter clearly didn't think this was strange.

She probably didn't think it was strange because these inert mannequin-creatures were everywhere now. Maya couldn't go anywhere without seeing one of the nauseating things in some stage of development.

By Christmas, Maya's parents were ensconced in hospital beds in the family living room. With IV drips in their arms, they lay with their hands linked, watching old movies while Maya ran around trying to keep up with the care. Their care and Elena's care.

Elena was sick now, too. She was the last of Maya's loved ones to get diagnosed. Jaxon and Noelle were dying. All Maya's cousins were dying. Mr. and Mrs. Davis were gone; the twins were on their own, and they were sick and dying. Mr. Thompson had already died, but Mrs. Thompson was hanging on, barely. She was dying, and now her children were sick and dying, too. Everyone was dying.

And the jelly-filled doll-babies were being born right and left, growing—it seemed—faster and faster with each passing day. Unsettling numbers of them had started showing up in public. They were amassing in parking lots, accumulating on street corners. They didn't move around. They just lay in clumps, like mounds of humanoid-looking debris, stacking up because no one was removing it. Maya couldn't understand why the mounds kept getting bigger and bigger. Where were they coming from?

A couple days before Christmas, Pastor Ben visited the house. When Maya opened the front door hesitantly (dreading that she'd find one of the new neighbor "children," aka doll-things, lying on the porch), she was beyond relieved to see her minister smiling at her as if he didn't have a care in the world.

Maya threw her arms around the broad-shouldered man with the unruly blond hair. "Pastor Ben! You're still alive!"

Maya hadn't been to church in months. When was

there time for church? Besides, she'd seen on the news that churches had been turned into clinics for the dying.

"Still kicking." Pastor Ben chuckled. "Apparently, it's not my time . . . yet."

Maya looked closely at Pastor Ben, and she realized he was sick, too. His skin had the same gray pallor she was seeing in everyone she knew and everyone she didn't know. He'd lost a lot of weight since she'd seen him last. He looked like a human hanger for his black shirt and slacks; his white liturgical collar was now two sizes too big for him.

Pretending that all was well, Maya opened the door and ushered Pastor Ben into the house. She motioned toward the living room, where her parents were weakly, but gamely, singing Christmas carols.

Pastor Ben smiled widely as he greeted Maya's mom and dad. "What a joyful noise!" he exclaimed.

As if it was perfectly normal, Pastor Ben grabbed a dining room chair and pulled it up next to Maya's dad's bed. Then he joined in the singing, adding his full baritone to Maya's mom's thready soprano and her dad's raspy tenor. Pastor Ben motioned to Maya, but she didn't have a single "fa la la la la" in her. She gave him a wan smile and said, "I've got to . . ." She ran from the room before she could finish.

She was in the kitchen making a peanut butter sandwich for Elena when Pastor Ben wandered in a few minutes later. She looked at him and dropped the knife she held.

"What's going on, Pastor Ben? Why is everyone dying?"

Pastor Ben lowered himself onto a kitchen chair. "It's not for us to ask why. We're given each day to live, not to question."

"But what about those things everywhere?" Maya asked.

Pastor Ben frowned in confusion. "Things?"

Maya gestured toward the street. "The jelly-people."

Pastor Ben still looked lost.

Maya threw up her hands, exasperated. "Those things that look like dolls made out of silicone inside plastic wrap!"

Pastor Ben shook his head. "The Lord doesn't distinguish life based on its appearance. All life is sacred."

"But those things are lifeless!" Maya shouted. "They're just—"

"Is that peanut butter?" Pastor Ben interrupted. "I could use a sandwich. It seems like I never have time to eat, what with all the funerals and baptisms."

Maya goggled at her minister. "You baptize those things?"

Pastor Ben smiled. "It's part of my job, Maya."

Maya shook her head. What more could she say? She felt like she was on a sinking ship and no one but her knew it was going down. No matter how much she ran around trying to sound the alarm, everyone continued to go about their business as if the world was as it should have been.

Sighing, Maya put the sandwich she'd been making for Elena on a saucer. She handed it to Pastor Ben. He patted her hand in thanks.

Lifting the sandwich, Pastor Ben said, "The world is

a paradox, Maya. A balance of good and bad. People are dying, yes, but life is proliferating. Not only are babies being born at an unprecedented rate, but they're also growing into adolescents and then adults in a manner of just days instead of years. Tragedies and miracles tend to go hand in hand."

Maya didn't even try to argue with Pastor Ben about his use of the word *babies*. He was seeing what he wanted; he was seeing what wasn't there.

Or maybe *she* was the one seeing what wasn't there? Were the jelly-beings real?

Yes, they had to be. Maya wasn't imaginative enough to conjure up those horrible things.

Over the next several days, Maya tried to find the miracles Pastor Ben had talked about. But it was hopeless. The minister was as delusional as everyone else.

One night, late, after Maya had cleaned up Elena's vomit, emptied her parents' bedpans, and sung her mother—whose pain was no longer manageable—to sleep, Maya went outside to her dormant flower garden.

Sitting on the little wooden bench her father had made for her a few years before, she stared at the brittle, bloomless stalks and tried to remember the lively colors that used to fill the yard in the summer. As soon as she tried to picture the flowers, she realized she was having trouble seeing color at all. Everything was so faded and gray now. The sick and the dying . . . they were hueless shells. And the new mannequin-things? They were sheer vessels, filled with nothing but limpid gel, like human-shaped jellyfish.

As she'd done many times since her world had started falling apart, Maya felt for her gold rose. She held it tightly as she leaned back and looked up at the constellations. Although the world beneath them no longer shone brightly, the stars still sparkled in the opaque expanse of the night sky.

Maya blinked as she looked at the stars. She inhaled sharply and sat up straight. The sparkle had triggered a memory, a reminder of the AR unit in the Pizzaplex.

That was when it had all started going wrong. Wasn't it?

Maya put a hand to her temple. The barely perceptible head pain that was a daily companion had begun the morning after she was in the AR booth. But what did that pain have to do with everything else?

Maya tried to remember when her gran was first diagnosed with cancer. She couldn't recall how long after her birthday it was when Gran got sick. She probably didn't remember because at the time, it wasn't noteworthy. Of course it was upsetting and sad, but it wasn't in any way peculiar.

What if . . . ?

"Maya?" a weak voice called out.

Maya let go of her gold rose pendant, jumped up, and dashed into the house. Was that her mom or Elena?

She ran first to her mom and found her asleep. She tore down the hall to her bedroom.

Elena was reaching for the plastic bin on the nightstand. Maya grabbed it and positioned it under Elena's chin. As she held her sister's hair while Elena threw up for the umpteenth time that day, Maya chastised herself for taking the time to sit outside. She didn't have the luxury of sitting under the stars. And she didn't have time to ask, "What if?"

All Maya had time for the next day and the next and the next was running from one sick family member or friend to the other. She no longer bothered to go to school. There were only a few classes available anyway.

She wouldn't have left the house at all if she could have helped it. She hated being out in the street. The jelly-mannequins were all over now. They seemed to be multiplying faster and faster. They cluttered up the stores and blocked the sidewalks. There were knots of them everywhere that Maya had to go.

And how did they get where they were? Maya had never seen one of the things move. They had limbs, but the limbs didn't seem to work. They could only lie around. They didn't talk, either. How could they? They didn't have mouths. They didn't have organs or blood or brains. They *weren't* human. They were just pretend humans, inexplicably growing objects that never grew into anything that actually functioned.

And they didn't just grow. They multiplied . . . on their own.

One day, on her way to Jaxon's house, Maya nearly crashed her bike when she saw one of the transparent creatures suddenly produce a smaller transparent creature. Maya wasn't close enough to the things—thankfully—to see clearly what happened, but it looked like the new, lank un-life slipped out of the larger one like an infant coming out the birth canal. Maya clapped a hand over her mouth to stifle a scream. How was this possible? The piles of jelly-beings were birthing more jelly-beings!

"Don't you think it's bizarre?" Maya asked Jaxon as she sat next to his bed one afternoon. She was trying to get him to swallow a protein drink.

Jaxon's parents had died weeks before. So had his older sister. He hadn't let that bother him. "I can take care of myself. We're all having to do that now, right?" After he'd buried his family, he'd gone on as if everything was hunky-dory. He still read his science and philosophy books. He still danced to music blasting from his boom box.

But then he got sick, too. He'd gone downhill fast.

Jaxon managed a sip of the vanilla protein shake Maya offered him, but he immediately spit it out. The sour vanilla odor made Maya's nose twitch.

Maya tried again, but Jaxon weakly pushed the bottle away. "What's bizarre?" he asked. His previously deep voice was barely audible, and it was scratchy, like his vocal cords were caught in brambles.

"All the . . . things out there." Maya waved her hand toward the street. As she turned that way, she caught a glimpse of several of the gossamer jelly-creatures piled up outside the window.

Jaxon looked toward the window and shrugged. "All experiences are valid." He coughed. Blood stained his lower lip.

Maya reached out and wiped Jaxon's mouth. She looked at the clock. She had to go home and check on Elena. But what about Jaxon? He could no longer take care of himself. Neither could Noelle. Her family was gone, too.

Maya had been racing from her house to Noelle's to Jaxon's to several of her neighbors' houses for days. Only her parents, her two youngest cousins, and her sister were left in her own family. She'd moved her cousins into her own house so she could watch over them.

"I have to go," Maya said. "I'm not sure my parents are going to last the rest of the day." Maya set the protein drink on Jaxon's nightstand. "Drink this when you can."

It occurred to her that she had just talked about her parents' imminent death without crying. She figured her tear ducts had dried up.

"I'll be back in the morning." Maya checked Jaxon's IV. She quickly replaced the bag dispensing his medication.

She might have run out of tears, Maya thought, *but she'd gained more nursing skills than she'd ever expected to have.* When she'd started caring for all her sick friends and relatives, she could barely handle the cleaning duties without getting sick herself. Now she could wipe up puke and pee and whatever else the body needed to expel without batting an eye. On top of that, she could now give painless shots and easily switch out IV catheters. Mrs. Thompson had taught her how to do that, before the woman got so sick she couldn't do anything at all.

Maya thought back to when she used to have dreams for her future. Sometimes she'd thought about being a doctor. Sometimes she'd thought about being a biologist or a botanist. Now she didn't think about being anything. All she could do was be there for the people she loved.

And she had to move if she was going to be there for everyone left in her care.

Maya leaned over and kissed Jaxon's forehead. One of his greasy locs brushed against her cheek.

"Don't worry about me," Jaxon rasped. "Go take care of your sister."

Jaxon's eyes fluttered closed; he was asleep. Maya adjusted his covers. Then she left his house. Skirting the jelly-people, she cycled back home.

By the time Maya returned to her house, she was shocked to find it nearly surrounded by mounds of the mannequin-things. There were so many of them in the road, on the sidewalks, and in the alley behind the house that they seemed to be more like one organism instead of several individual sacks of translucent jelly.

Maya barely managed to squeeze past a conglomeration of the things to get in her front door. Inside, she slammed the door closed and bolted it. Then she ran to the front window and dropped the blinds.

It was only after plunging the room into total darkness that she turned to check on her parents. And she realized she wasn't hearing what she should have been hearing.

For the past few days, her parents' breathing had been phlegmy and labored. They inhaled as if sucking through a straw, and they exhaled in a watery rattle that Maya could barely stand to listen to. The sound of their struggle to get air had been relentless. It had seemed to echo through the house, reaching Maya no matter where she was or what she was doing.

But now that sound was gone.

Maya switched on a lamp and crossed to her mom's

side. Her mom was still, her eyes open and glazed. Maya gently closed her mother's eyes.

Shifting her gaze to her dad, Maya saw that his eyes were already closed. But he was just as motionless. He was gone, too.

Maya wanted to linger by her parents' side, but she didn't have time. She'd been gone too long. She needed to check her sister and her cousins.

"I love you, Mom and Dad," she whispered. Then she ran to her parents' bedroom.

Maya had put her youngest cousins in her parents' queen-sized bed. She'd surrounded them with pillows, so they couldn't fall out of the bed. Now she picked up Axel and held him close. His cheeks were no longer pudgy. He hadn't smiled in a long time. But he was still accepting milk or juice from his favorite froggy sippy cup.

Maya quickly got the cup and nudged the cup's opening into Axel's slack mouth. As she urged him to drink, she checked on his sister, Abril, who was five. Abril had always been a tornado of a child, whirling constantly because she loved to dance, or whipping from one activity to the other. She'd never been able to stay still. Now Abril barely moved. Her usual perky and shiny pigtails were limp and lusterless. Maya had wanted to wash Abril's hair for days, but feeding Abril and her brother and the others Maya had left to care for took precedence.

"Abril, *niña*," Maya said.

The little girl's eyes fluttered open.

"Can you eat something?" Continuing to hold the sippy cup for Axel, Maya tried to hand a small container of pudding to Abril. Abril closed her eyes and screwed up her face. She shook her head.

At the same time, Axel reared back from the sippy cup and threw up all over Maya's chest. Maya quickly settled the boy in the bed and made sure he hadn't aspirated any of the vomit. She cleaned him up as best she could and then hurried to the bathroom.

Pulling off her shirt, Maya washed herself off. She left the bathroom and headed toward her bedroom. Grabbing a T-shirt from the back of the door, she pulled it on. She made a face when she got a whiff of sweat. This shirt wasn't much cleaner than the one she'd just taken off. But she was out of clean clothes. She hadn't had time to do laundry in . . . she couldn't remember the last time.

Elena, lying limply in her bed, moaned. Maya rushed to her side.

Checking the IV stand, she saw that Elena's intravenous bag was empty. She was in pain.

Maya reached for a new bag. That's when she realized there wasn't one. She'd forgotten to restock the supplies. She had to go back out.

When it had become clear that medical personnel couldn't keep up with all the sick and dying people, the government had set up chemotherapy dispensaries in every town. If you had insurance, you could just pick up the medication and administer it yourself instead of going to the chemo wards . . . if you were well enough to get it.

Maya was the only one left in her family and in her neighborhood who was strong enough to go anywhere.

The last time she'd been to the dispensary, she'd tried to stock up with enough for everyone she was helping. Obviously, she hadn't gotten enough.

After giving Elena as much water as she'd accept and trying—unsuccessfully—to give Axel and Abril more food, Maya had grabbed the car keys and headed into the garage. The dispensary was too far away for a bike ride. And besides, the jelly-people made bike rides harrowing.

It wasn't that these partially formed humanoid sacks were dangerous. As far as Maya had been able to tell, the empty beings that looked like vaguely human-shaped clear water balloons were benign. They didn't have enough substance to be malevolent. And even if they were, what could they do? They couldn't move.

But their existence was enough to creep out Maya. The things, in their very wrongness, sent shivers skittering along Maya's spine. Because they were so unnatural, the doll-people unsettled Maya. And if she stopped to think about it, Maya fully expected them to become a threat sooner or later. The sheer volume of them was chilling. How long would it be before they covered the entire surface of the planet?

She made sure she didn't stop to think about that very often.

In the garage, Maya started her family's minivan before she hit the garage door opener. If the jelly-people were heaped in the driveway, Maya didn't want to risk them spilling into the garage before she could get the van going.

Maya barely waited for the garage door to clear the top of the van before she put it in reverse and hit the gas. As she'd feared, several of the eerie mannequin-things were in the driveway. Well, she'd plow right over them if she needed to.

Maya backed hard out of the garage and hit the opener button again. Because her gaze was on the road behind her, Maya wasn't sure if any of the jelly-things slopped into her garage. She figured if they did, she'd deal with that later.

Once she had the van in the street, it was relatively easy to navigate through the collections of dummy-sacks. Besides the mannequin-things, the streets were mostly empty. Nearly everyone was either sick or at home taking care of the sick. Maya only saw a few cars as she navigated through town. The rest were parked in their driveways or tucked into their garages. Some were in parking lots, but most of the lots were empty. People were dying, but they weren't dropping dead where they stood. That was what was weird about everything. It wasn't like a zombie apocalypse or anything. There wasn't a virus or a killing chemical released by a foreign country. It was cancer, and although the disease was killing people quickly, everyone had time to get to a hospital or to their home to die. That was why Maya's community now looked like a ghost town—quite literally.

The doll-things, if you ignored their odd jelly consistency and the fact that they didn't go anywhere, were uncannily similar to specters. But Maya knew they weren't ghosts. They weren't . . . well, they weren't *anything* actually. They had no heart, no emotion. They had no spirit. They were like globs of nothingness in plastic containers, like human leftovers.

When Maya had first seen Cecilia, the baby's head had reminded Maya of her family's dinner rolls, but now she saw the jelly-things as more uncooked dough than a finished product of any kind. They were like batter waiting to go in the oven and get baked.

Nearing the dispensary, Maya's way was blocked by a ROAD UNDER CONSTRUCTION sign. She started to make a right turn to detour around it, but then she braked and stared at the sign. What was with all the UNDER CONSTRUCTION signs she'd been seeing? Maya frowned, her mind flipping back to other such signs . . . starting with the one that had been in front of the AR unit.

She tapped her fingers on the steering wheel as she tried to attach meaning to how often she'd seen such signs. Her brain, however, couldn't come up with any coherent ideas about it. Finally, she shrugged and shook her head. She got the car moving again.

Maya was able to drive the rest of the way to the dispensary without incident. There, it was a bit more challenging to avoid the aggregations of jelly-things to get into the flat-roofed industrial building, but she managed it.

There was only one woman left on duty behind the desk. She didn't appear to be much older than Maya. She might have been a college student before all this had started. And she'd probably been pretty. Now she was obviously sick herself; her eyes were sunken, and her complexion was the color of ash. Brushing a strand of oily brown hair from her face, the woman waved away Maya's attempt to fill out the right paperwork.

"Just take what you need." The woman's voice was barely a whisper, like tissue paper rustling in an air current.

Maya didn't argue. She filled the tote bags she'd brought with her with as many intravenous bags of medication as she could stuff into them. Then she rushed out of the building.

In the parking lot, Maya was shocked to see that several piles of jelly-people now ringed the outermost rows. Had they been there when she'd arrived? Had she just not noticed them?

Maya didn't stop to consider the question because one large pyramid of the jelly-people was now close to the minivan. She ran to the vehicle, threw in the tote bags, and slammed the door shut. She had the engine turned over and the van in gear just as several new jelly-beings tumbled off the nearest pile and landed near the front bumper. She backed up fast and tore out of the parking lot.

Purposefully, Maya kept her gaze straight ahead. She was not going to look in the rearview mirror to see what was behind her.

On the way home, Maya considered stopping by the grocery store. She'd filled the kitchen with canned soups, cartons of pudding, and bottles of protein drinks, but she figured she should add to what she had. When she got to the store, though, the parking lot was nearly buried by the jelly-things. They were everywhere, like jiggly container-less gelatin. She couldn't face even trying to make her way through the quivering mass.

She headed back to her neighborhood.

Maya's street was thick with the pellucid creatures when she reached it. She gazed down the road to her house. It looked like her driveway had turned into a massive heap of Jell-O. She looked to her right.

The van was idling in front of the Thompsons' house, and only a few of the mannequin-things were lying around the two-story structure. Maya was trying to take care of the last surviving member of the family, Donny. She figured she might as well leave the car there and run in to check on him. She could hopefully jog home behind the houses, keeping away from as many jelly-people as possible.

Maya pulled into the Thompsons' driveway. She quickly got out of the car, slinging her tote bags of medicine across her body. Running around behind the house, she let herself in the back door, closed it, and locked it behind her.

"Donny, it's me!" she called out.

A weak groan answered her.

Maya set the totes on the cluttered kitchen table. She sighed as she glanced around the dirty, neglected room. Gone were the shining surfaces and well-ordered pans and utensils she was used to seeing in Mrs. Thompson's domain. The sink was piled with dishes. The granite counters were smeared with stains—Maya didn't want to think about what fluids they were. The room smelled putrid, like spoiled food.

Maya tried to remember sitting in the Thompsons' kitchen eating snickerdoodles and listening to Mr.

Thompson's bad knock-knock jokes. Maya could almost hear him now.

"Knock, knock."

"Who's there?"

"Cancer."

"Cancer who?"

"Cancer see I'm busy?"

That had been the last joke he'd told her. She'd forced herself to pretend laugh. And she cried copiously when he'd pressed an envelope full of cash into her hand. "Take care of the kids until child services arrive?" he'd asked pleadingly.

Maya had nodded. She didn't have the heart to tell him that child services couldn't keep up with all the orphaned kids. She'd take care of Donny, Parker, and Aurora until the end.

As she reached into the fridge for a fruit cup now, Maya wondered if the memories of her happy times in this room had really been in this lifetime. It seemed like it had happened to another Maya, maybe in one of those parallel realities Jaxon used to like to talk about.

Maya froze with one hand in the fridge. Parallel reality. *Was* this real?

She returned to the what-if question that had been nagging her ever since she'd looked up at the stars. What if this *wasn't* real?

After all, how *could* it be real? Everyone dying of cancer? The streets filled with fast-growing jelly-beings?

What if she was still in the AR booth?

If she was, how could she tell?

She thought back to her big, augmented birthday bash.

When she'd partied with the crowd of well-wishers, it hadn't felt virtual at all. It had seemed as real as anything else she'd ever experienced. So how did she know whether *this* was real?

Maya grabbed a fruit cup and pulled her hand from the fridge. She closed the fridge door with a muted *whump*. The fridge hummed, and Maya remained where she was, mesmerized by the sound . . . until a *thud* came from the back of the house.

Maya jerked herself out of her trance, quickly grabbed a bag of medicine from the tote, and trotted out of the kitchen. It had sounded like Donny had fallen out of bed. She hurried to his room.

Sure enough, Donny was on the floor.

"What are you doing down there, bud?" Maya asked him brightly as if his face wasn't contorted in pain, as if his lips weren't cracked, and as if he wasn't as skeletal as a cadaver.

Donny mumbled something that sounded like "brr," but she knew he was trying to tell her he'd dropped "Bert," his stuffed alligator. Maya picked up the fallen spittle-encrusted plush toy. Then she effortlessly lifted what was left of the rambunctious little boy she used to play hide-and-seek with.

"Can you eat some fruit?" she asked, holding up the fruit cup.

Donny shook his head. Maya sighed and switched out his intravenous bag.

She glanced at her watch as she did. She had to get back home. Elena had been without meds for too long.

And she had to try and get something in Abril and Axel. On the way, she should check on the Davis twins.

Maya set the fruit cup on Donny's nightstand. She tucked Bert under Donny's lax arm. "I'll be back, kiddo," she told him.

He blinked up at her. His eyes shifted, as if he was realizing who she was. For a second, his face looked more animated. Weakly, he lifted a hand and pointed across the room.

Maya turned and scanned the shelves that hugged the wall opposite Donny's bed. What was he pointing at?

"Prsss," Donny said.

Maya glanced at his face. His expression was intense. He was determined that she understood.

Maya crossed to the shelves. And she saw it. There was a clumsily wrapped package with her name on it on the shelf.

With a shaking hand, she picked it up. A piece of red folded construction paper was taped to the package. She opened the paper and read: "Happy Birthday, Maya!" She recognized Donny's large, crooked lettering.

Maya looked back at Donny. He was watching her with more attentiveness than she'd seen in him for days. She returned to his bed and opened the package.

Pulling out a "vase"—a tin can sprayed with gold and decorated with gold-painted rocks, she discovered that her tears hadn't dried up after all. They spilled from her eyes and cascaded down her cheeks as she looked at Donny's strained but eager face.

"This is beautiful!" she exclaimed.

Donny blinked. Then he closed his eyes, satisfied.

Maya realized the gift must have been sitting there since her seventeenth non-birthday. He'd probably forgotten about it. Why had he remembered it now?

Wiping her eyes, Maya leaned over and kissed Donny's forehead. She held the vase against her heart, and she left the room.

Back in the kitchen, Maya splashed water on her face. She grabbed her tote bags, tucking the vase in with the medicine. She glanced out the kitchen window and tensed when she saw how many more jelly-people were in the Thompsons' front yard. She was going to have to sneak out the back door and go down the alley. She slipped into the utility room off the kitchen and gingerly cracked open the door.

Maya exhaled in relief. The Thompsons' backyard was empty of the mannequin-things. She stepped out of the house and closed and locked the door behind her. Trotting to the back of the property, she eased into the alley.

She froze. Here, the way wasn't so clear. The alley was thick with the clear-skinned creatures. There would be no way to avoid them completely. They didn't form a solid mass, though. Maya figured she'd be able to weave her way around them. She took a deep breath, and she took off at a fast jog.

Six houses stood between the Thompsons' house and Maya's home. The first one belonged to Mr. Vance, the mean old man who kicked his dog. Maya glanced in his back window as she passed it, and she nearly stumbled when she saw him watching her. He was still alive? She'd thought all the old people were dead. *The man was probably too ornery to die*, she thought, as she picked up her pace.

The Davis twins were two doors down from her. It only took her a few seconds to get to their back fence. Unfortunately, though, the back of the Davis house was surrounded by the see-through-skins. Maya's pace faltered. Should she try it?

Studying the creatures around the Davis house, Maya thought she saw a path through them. But then, as she watched, the path disappeared.

The things were reproducing faster and faster now, right before Maya's eyes. This was as close as she'd ever been to them when they'd churned out more of themselves. She could actually see their jiggling masses convulsing before ejecting new smaller versions of themselves. They did this over and over. They were . . . spawning.

No, she couldn't risk going into the Davis house. She needed to get to Elena and her cousins sooner rather than later. The twins would have to wait. Maya picked up her pace again.

Maya dodged around a horde of jelly-creatures. Then she ran full out to the back of her house. There, she was dismayed to see that her beloved garden was buried in the gelatinous people-things. There was barely enough room for her to zip past them and get in her back door.

As she passed the last of the creatures before fumbling the door open, she brushed against it. The cold, oily feel of the thing's skin made her shudder. Bile rose up in the back of her throat. She swallowed it down and slammed the back door closed. She bolted it and leaned against its solid wood panels, her chest heaving.

For several seconds, Maya couldn't move. Her own limbs felt as insubstantial as those of the things outside her door.

A faint cry coming from her parents' room got her going again.

"I'm coming!" she called. She couldn't tell if it was Axel or Abril who had cried out.

When she got into the room, she realized it was Abril. Axel was unconscious, his little fists curled tightly around the top of the dirty blanket that covered him. Maya cringed at the sight of the filth. She had to find time to wash linens and get everyone cleaned up.

Rushing to Abril's side, Maya dropped the totes and picked up the pudding container she'd left for the little girl. It hadn't been opened, of course. Abril thrashed in the bed, a painful grimace on her face.

Maya grabbed Abril and wrapped her in a hug. "I'm here, *niña*. I'm here."

Abril moaned and cried out again. Maya brushed Abril's wet, matted hair from her clammy forehead. She rocked the child in her arms and started humming a lullaby.

Maya wasn't sure how long she hummed and rocked. Quite a while, she decided, when she realized that one of her arms had gone numb from supporting Abril's weight. Maya eased her cousin back onto the bed. Then she looked over at Axel.

Axel's fists were no longer clenched. His little hands were slack. So was his face. He was gone.

Maya closed her eyes, waiting for the tears to flow again. They didn't come. Maybe she'd used up her reserves when she'd seen Donny's gift.

Opening her eyes, Maya leaned over and kissed Axel's already-cooling skin. "Good-bye, my sweet boy," she whispered.

Her spirit as numb as her arm, Maya stood. She turned and left her parents' bedroom. Straightening her shoulders, she headed down the hall to check on Elena. Would she be gone, too?

Would it be so bad if she was?

Just outside her doorway, Maya sank to the floor. She closed her eyes and let her head fall back against the wall with a *thunk*. She barely felt the impact.

She couldn't do it anymore. Who was she kidding? There was no way she could keep up with trying to feed and medicate the people that were left for her to care for. What was the point? Everyone was going to die.

Everyone but Maya.

Maya opened her eyes. Why wasn't she getting sick? Why did it seem to be happening to everyone around her? It was as if she was at the focal point of everything.

Just like she had been at her big birthday party.

Maybe she *was* still in the AR unit.

Maya touched her forehead, where the faint pain was still discernable. She'd been far too busy to pay attention to it, but it was there. Was it there because the headband was still in place?

Maya shook her head. No, this was all just too . . . intense to be part of some kind of computer-generated scenario.

But why was it happening?

Had the AR booth somehow augmented the whole world? Or had she jumped into a parallel universe?

Maya sighed. She didn't know enough to answer these questions. Probably no one did.

Maya stood.

She had to stop feeling sorry for herself. And she still needed to check on Elena. Even if Elena was going to die, she deserved as much comfort as Maya could offer until then.

Maya glanced at the bedroom window as she crossed to Elena's bed. And she wished she hadn't.

Just in the time she'd spent in the hallway, the jelly-beings outside her house had multiplied alarmingly. A mountain of them was pressing against the house, as if trying to merge with the dwelling.

Maya stared at the fragile glass covering the window. Maybe the threat she'd felt sidling along with the jelly-creatures had finally arrived.

But what could she do about it?

Maya decided to play ostrich. Out of sight, out of mind. She turned her back to the window and went to her sister's side.

Elena was so still that Maya thought she was gone. She felt her sister's fragile wrist. No, Elena was alive. Barely. A faint pulse fluttered against her thin skin.

Without looking at the window, Maya reached into one of the tote bags and pulled out a bag of medicine. She hooked it up and checked the rate of the drip.

She wasn't sure why she was bothering. Elena was

obviously unconscious, and she would probably pass away without waking up. But Maya needed to feel like she was doing *something.*

Maya was starting to lie down on the bed next to her sister when the window behind her shattered. Maya spun around as a series of loud cracks and clatters sounded throughout the house.

She screamed.

The jelly-beings were no longer pressing against the house. They were pouring *into* the house through the broken windows. Sloshing through the jagged opening like a transparent octopus with an infinite number of legs, the aggregation of viscous humanoids was more liquid than solid. They flowed into the room as if they were a ghastly jellyfish-filled tsunami surging up onto the beach.

Maya whirled toward Elena. She bent over to lift her sister, but she realized immediately that Elena was no longer breathing. Her hardly there pulse was gone.

Maya didn't want to leave her sister's body in the room, but when something slick started to encircle Maya's ankle, she couldn't think anymore. All she could do was react. She turned and ran from the room.

Barreling down the hall, Maya careened around the corner toward the kitchen. She didn't have a solid plan in her head, but some part of her mind thought that if she could get to the garage, she would be safe. The garage had no windows, and both the garage door and the main door were thick and strong. How long could she hold out in there? She didn't think that far ahead. All she wanted to do now was get away from the squishy mass of gel-humanoids.

She'd always thought the things were mindless. But now she wondered. Did they have intention? If they did, what did they want?

Maya glanced into the kitchen. She gasped. The kitchen was filled with the creatures. She looked to her left. So was the living room. All the windows in the house were shattered. The front door had been smashed open. The doll-things were tumbling toward her from all directions.

Even though each individual jelly-thing didn't take action on its own—except to push out more jelly-things—the congregation of them created movement. They were like specks of dirt—one of them might be harmless, but combined together, they had enough weight and force to bury her if they cascaded over her.

If the things did have an intention, it was a communal one, and it didn't appear to be a good one. They were slowly but surely surrounding her.

Maya lunged for the door leading out to the garage. She flung it open and leaped into the darkness before slamming the door closed behind her.

Instantly, she realized her mistake.

When she'd left the house earlier, she hadn't closed the garage door fast enough. Some of the creatures had obviously fallen in before the door had come down.

Maya was overtaken by a squishy, cold, slimy mass. The sensation was disgusting—it felt like she'd thrown herself into a bowl of sticky rice noodles.

The jelly-beings filled the garage. And now they incorporated Maya as if she was an essential missing part of their collective. They entwined around her, merging with her. Smothering her.

Seeking comfort and strength, Maya groped for her gold rose. When she found it, she clenched her fist around it, trying to fill herself with the love it represented. If only it was a magic rose, like ruby shoes that could transport her back to . . .

Maya's mouth and nose filled with the malleable mush of the creatures that embraced her. She struggled to get air, expecting each breath to be her last.

But her last breath didn't come.

The spongy, ever-expanding weight burgeoned above her, and it felt like her body wouldn't be able to take the pressure any longer. But it did.

Maya couldn't see anything. She couldn't hear or smell anything. She'd gone beyond feeling, too. All she was aware of was the force above her, and even that was becoming too much for her mind to comprehend.

Why wasn't she dead yet?

When would this be over?

Maya tried to inhale and couldn't. Hopefully, this would end soon.

Or would it?

ABOUT THE AUTHORS

Scott Cawthon is the author of the bestselling video game series *Five Nights at Freddy's*, and while he is a game designer by trade, he is first and foremost a storyteller at heart. He is a graduate of The Art Institute of Houston and lives in Texas with his family.

Kelly Parra is the author of YA novels *Graffiti Girl, Invisible Touch*, and other supernatural short stories. In addition to her independent works, Kelly works with Kevin Anderson & Associates on a variety of projects. She resides in Central Coast, California, with her husband and two children.

Andrea Rains Waggener is an author, novelist, ghostwriter, essayist, short story writer, screenwriter, copywriter, editor, poet, and a proud member of Kevin Anderson & Associates' team of writers. In a past she prefers not to remember much, she was a claims adjuster, JCPenney's catalog order-taker (before computers!), appellate court clerk, legal writing instructor, and lawyer. Writing in genres that vary from her chick-lit novel, *Alternate Beauty*, to her dog how-to book, *Dog Parenting*, to her self-help book, *Healthy, Wealthy, & Wise*, to ghostwritten memoirs to ghostwritten YA, horror, mystery, and mainstream fiction projects, Andrea still manages to find time to watch the rain and obsess over her dog and her knitting, art, and music projects. She lives with her husband and said dog on the Washington Coast, and if she isn't at home creating something, she can be found walking on the beach.

Gil grunted as he struggled to free a battered metal endoskeleton from beneath the edge of the warped wooden stage. Sweat that saturated his hair and forehead dripped from his left eyebrow into his eye. The salty liquid stung. Gil swore, released his grip on the endoskeleton's ankle, and wiped his eye.

"We're never going to get out of here," Gil grumbled. He straightened and turned to survey the dingy ruins of the old pizzeria he and his coworkers were charged with renovating.

Gil didn't know how old the place was, but it definitely had seen better days. It was filthy and littered with trash and scrap, most of which consisted of discarded animatronic endoskeletons—heavy metal robotic parts that were a bear to lift and transport. Gil was sick of dragging the things around.

Gil reached for the water bottle he'd left on the edge of the stage. He took a swig and gazed at the seemingly endless work that lay ahead of him. Robotic endoskeletons—the vaguely human-skeleton-shaped steel frameworks over which all of Fazbear Enterprises animatronics were built—were piled everywhere. The place looked like the aftermath of a robotic Armageddon. Not only was the old pizzeria bulging with discarded metal skeletons, it was also filled with broken-down tables and chairs and red-vinyl-topped stools, stacks of wooden beams and cement blocks, and piles of concrete and metal rubble. Weirdly, bright blue and green and red plates and cups, along with purple-striped tablecloths, were strewn among the larger debris.

This part of the pizzeria was its main dining room—a large red-walled room dominated by a rectangular stage. Although the pizzeria's electrical systems were mostly shot and Gil and his teammates had to set up work lights around the room, the stage lights—for reasons no one understood—always shone brightly. A row of the round, piercing lights lined the front of the stage and also encircled a smaller, semicircular stage next to the large one. On either end of the big stage, more of the floodlights glared out from rows of old speakers that sat silently, their black surfaces obscured by who knew how many years of grime.

Just as Gil set down his water bottle and prepared to lean over the stuck endoskeleton, Danny, the eager beaver twenty-year-old who drove Gil nuts with his constant cheerful chatter and "isn't this fun?" attitude, crawled out from underneath the stage. Danny brought a cloud of dust with him. Gil wrinkled his nose at the fetid smell that wafted from under the stage's cracked front skirting.

Danny squirmed across the black-and-white-checked linoleum floor and scooted away from the stage. He held the end of a rope that was tied to another endoskeleton and dragged the broken-down robotic frame behind him. It slid out easily, not caught on anything like the one Gil was dealing with.

"This is the last one from way under the stage," Danny said. "It's so cool under there!"

"Cool?" Gil curled his lip. "Only if you like filth and cobwebs." He snorted and waved a hand to indicate the whole room they were in. "There's nothing cool about this place."

Danny sprang to his feet. He brushed off his perfectly creased khakis and his equally perfectly pressed denim shirt.

Who ironed a denim shirt? Gil wondered.

Danny looked and acted like a momma's boy; his precisely combed blond hair and too-cute face went with his merry attitude, his stories about his beloved mother, and his obsession with following rules. Even though Gil was just a few years older than Danny, Gil thought of Danny as a kid.

Gil was Danny's opposite. Since he never wore anything but jeans and T-shirts, Gil had never ironed a thing in his twenty-four years on the planet. He didn't even like his mom, and he avoided rules like the plague. Gil also would never be described as cute—he liked to think of himself as rugged . . . and bad. Gil was one of those guys women claimed to hate but secretly wanted; they couldn't resist his shaggy brown hair, unshaven face, and brooding dark brown eyes.

Gil shook his head. This job wouldn't be over fast enough to suit him. And not just because of working with guys like Danny.

"There's too much work here for just the four of us," Gil said. He looked across the room toward the other two men on the renovation team; Owen and Carlo were working together to add yet another endoskeleton to a growing stack near the only exit from the old pizzeria. All the other doors and windows in the place were obstructed by heavy lumber and cement blocks.

"No way we're going to get everything done by the deadline they've given us," Gil continued. "The suits have no idea how hard it is to break down these things." Gil gestured toward the endoskeleton Danny was now dragging across the floor.

"If you'd stop complaining so much, the work would go a lot faster," Danny said.

Gil gave Danny a dirty look, which Danny ignored.

Danny kept talking. "These endoskeletons are fascinating," he said. "And we're getting good exercise. It's like being paid to work out." He flexed an admittedly impressive bicep and grinned. "Plus, I think it's great how we're going to renovate this place back to how it was in its heyday. I heard they're thinking about not only sprucing it up and preserving it but maybe even memorializing it, like turning it into a museum or something. I think it's awesome that they're building the new Pizzaplex above this old place. It's really an honor to be part of this kind of project."

Gil rolled his eyes and turned his back on Danny. "I'm going outside to get some fresh air," Gil said.

"But you just took a break about fifteen minutes ago," Danny said.

"Yeah, well, I'm taking another one. Deal with it." Gil headed toward the old pizzeria's only exit.

Watching a downpour so heavy it looked like a gray curtain instead of individual water drops, Theo huddled next to his coworker and friend Bryce, a tall, skinny guy who was a lot stronger than he looked. They both were attempting to shelter under metal scaffolding, which wasn't up to the task of keeping them dry.

Rain spattered Theo's heavy work boots as he frowned at the big delivery truck that was backing toward him with a shrill *beep-beep-beep* that cut through the crackling and drumming sounds of the rain. Theo coughed and turned away from the truck's smelly exhaust. Bryce covered his nose and shook his head.

"What's with the delivery?" Bryce asked. "We haven't even enclosed anything yet."

Theo shrugged. He and Bryce had been part of the construction team working on Freddy Fazbear's Mega Pizzaplex for several weeks—long enough for Theo to learn that asking questions was never a good idea. Theo thought that a lot of what went on at the Pizzaplex was strange—like building a modern entertainment complex over the remains of an old pizzeria, for instance. But Theo didn't care. The pay was great, and the gig was a long one. Even after all this time, the Pizzaplex was still in its fledgling stage; it currently looked like a giant dome-shaped metal cage. Theo and his team, and all the other workers on the project, were just finishing up setting the rebar and concrete that would make up the skeletal structure of the building.

The truck came to a stop, and a big curly-haired guy jumped out of the cab. Sheltering a clipboard under a lightweight jacket that was rain saturated within seconds, the man ran toward Theo and Bryce.

Theo stepped back to make room for the man, who smelled of sweat and spearmint. The man, popping the gum he chewed vigorously, nodded a thanks and shook himself like a dog. Theo and Bryce were both sprayed.

Theo pointed at the man's clipboard. "Do I need to sign?"

The man nodded and presented the clipboard to Theo. A gust of wind blew the rain under the scaffolding, and the paper on the clipboard fluttered. Theo quickly scanned the wet page. He raised an eyebrow. *State-of-the-art animatronics?* Bryce was right. It was weird to be receiving these now, when the building was little more than an open framework. But Theo had been told that his team was supposed to receive and unload this shipment. So, he signed the delivery order.

"Thanks," the big man said. He popped his gum, turned, and ran back toward the truck's cab. He tossed the clipboard inside, then trotted to the back of the truck. The man flipped a big metal latch; it made a metallic *thunk*. Then he threw up the door, which ratcheted open with a series of squeaks and thuds.

The man stepped back under the scaffolding. Together, he and Theo and Bryce looked into the back of the truck.

Bryce gasped.

"Whoa," the man said. He stopped chewing his gum.

Theo frowned. "The delivery order said 'new state-of-the-art animatronics.'" He pointed. "So what happened to that one?"

The man shook his head. He strode forward and jumped up into the back of the truck. Theo exchanged a look with Bryce, then followed the man. Bryce stayed where he was.

The inside of the truck was dark and smelled like sawdust and motor oil. Rain pounding on the truck's metal roof was amplified in the small space; it sounded like several people were banging on the top of the truck with hammers.

Theo and the truck driver studied a collection of friendly-looking animatronics. Theo's gaze shifted from one robot to the next. All of them were gleaming in brand-new perfection . . . all of them except one.

This animatronic was anything but bright and shiny and friendly-looking. "What could have done this?" Theo asked.

The truck driver shook his head and shuffled his feet nervously. "I got no idea."

Theo shook his head. "Well, they're going to need another guitarist."

As soon as the back of the truck opened up, Gil left the shelter of the cement half-wall where he liked to take his breaks. The wall was a few feet from the exterior framework of the Pizzaplex, and none of the construction workers had a problem with him hanging out there.

Now, though, Gil stepped up beside the tall, thin guy who waited under the scaffolding. The guy didn't notice Gil at first. He was looking toward the big truck driver and the other guy, a broad-shouldered thirtysomething man with a receding hairline. Actually, the tall guy was looking beyond the driver and the prematurely balding man. He was looking at the stripped-down robot.

Gil looked at the robot, too. Grinning, he dashed through the rain and hopped up into the back of the truck. The men in the truck turned to look at him.

"Hey." Gil stuck out a hand toward the guy with too much forehead. "Gil."

"Theo." Theo shook Gil's hand, but he was frowning, clearly wondering what Gil was doing there.

"I'm part of the reno crew," Gil explained. He pointed at the bare endoskeleton. "I'll take that one."

Theo cocked his head.

Gil didn't give Theo a chance to form a question. Gil stepped toward the seven-foot metal skeleton. He gripped its arm. "This obviously isn't going to be used for whatever those are for." He gestured at the new, undamaged animatronics. "But it looks strong and sturdy. I think I can repurpose it and use it to break down and pile up all the heavy, trashed endoskeletons we're trying to clear out of the old pizzeria."

"I don't think—" Theo began.

Gil bumped Theo, forcing him to step back. Theo frowned but didn't stop Gil as he tipped the bare endoskeleton forward and began dragging it across the aluminum truck bed.

The metal-on-metal screech warred with the rain's continued drubbing.

Gil made sure the endoskeleton brushed against Theo, and he grinned when Theo jumped back even farther. Gil knew his six-foot-two frame and his "just try me" face would be enough to intimidate Theo into silence. Just to be sure, though, he glared a challenge at Theo.

Theo raised both hands in a gesture of surrender. "Have at it," Theo said.

Gil jumped out into the rain and dragged his prize off the truck.

By the time Gil managed to drag the endoskeleton into the old pizzeria, he was panting and sweating heavily. But he didn't care. This thing was going to make Gil's life much, much easier.

Gil laid the robot against one of the side walls of the pizzeria's dining room. He straightened and wiped his face with the back of his hand.

"What the heck are you doing?" Carlo stepped up beside Gil and scowled at the barebones robot. He too wiped his face; his dark skin glistened with sweat, and moisture beaded up on the oak leaf tattoo on his forearm. "We're supposed to be getting them out, not bringing them in."

Gil looked down at Carlo and clapped the short but sturdy guy on the back. "This is going to do exactly that."

Carlo frowned in confusion.

Gil laughed. He looked at the stripped-down animatronic. "Stay there," he said to the robot. "I'll be right back."

Gil ignored Carlo's baffled and exasperated look and strode across the room to what used to be the arcade part of the pizzeria. In the narrow aisles between dark and broken arcade games, Gil and his coworkers left their personal belongings during the day. The old pizzeria's employee area was too filled with rubbish to use, and the temporary trailers set up outside the Pizzaplex's construction zone were earmarked for the construction crew, not the renovation crew. Of course. The reno crew was treated like second-class citizens . . . but not for long. Gil was going to change that.

Gil found his backpack next to Danny's shiny red lunch pail (Danny was such a little boy), and he quickly reached into it and pulled out his laptop. Finally, Gil was going to show the suits they'd been wrong to stick him on this crew, doing the grunt work.

When Gil had applied for a job at the Pizzaplex, he'd thought he'd be chosen as part of the tech team. He didn't have any actual work experience as a programmer, but he tinkered with programs—and robotics—all the time at home. He'd told the suits what an asset he'd be, but they didn't believe him. And he'd ended up down in this hole, dragging around old dead robots.

But not anymore.

Gil hurried back to the prone endoskeleton. Carlo had moved off. He and Owen were now struggling to break down one of the endoskeletons stacked by the stage. Owen's bowling-ball-round face was flushed red with exertion.

"Suckers," Gil muttered. He opened his laptop and set it on the floor. Then he knelt next to his new worker robot.

Whereas the endoskeletons Gil and his teammates had been hauling and dismantling were just metal versions of a human's skeletal system, this endoskeleton was more substantial. It wasn't just a basic metal structure; its steel frame was contained within a bulging collection of metal rods and curved plates and an impressive system of ball joints and pistons. All of this was topped with a long, vaguely rectangular-shaped shiny steel skull. The skull was the only part of the endoskeleton that was shiny. The rest was dark and discolored, as if it had survived some kind of fire. The upper part of the shiny skull contained bulging white eyes encased in steel sockets, and the lower part contained a hinged, metal-toothed mouth. Jutting from the top of the head, a pair of bent metal ears stuck out like antennae.

Feeling around the back of the base of the metallic skull, Gil found a small switch. He pressed it, and the robot's jaw shifted forward with a faint whir. The jaw clicked into a full-open position, revealing a mass of circuits, chips, and wires within the skull. Gil probed the wires and found the one that ıad a power coupler. He gently pulled it out and connected it with his laptop.

As soon as the animatronic was linked to Gil's computer, ts specs and operating systems code scrolled down the laptop creen. Gil leaned forward and scanned the code. When he aw what he was looking for, he reached out and tapped a few keys.

"Cleanup protocol. Check." Gil's gaze shifted from his laptop to the robot and back again to the screen.

After a few seconds, the screen prompted: *Protocol uploaded.*

Gil disconnected his laptop from the robot. He started to reach for the animatronic jaw, but he paused when a shadow fell over the keyboard. He looked up.

Danny, looking as clean and fresh as he had at the start of the day, was staring at the endoskeleton. "What are you doing?" Danny asked. "I didn't think any of these things worked."

"This is a new one," Gil said. "I've activated a cleanup protocol."

Gil reached out and pushed the robot's jaw back into place. As soon as the whir and click ended, the white eyes glowed orange. The robot's joints hummed and hissed as it sat up.

Danny yelped. Gil grinned when Danny took several stutter steps backward. Out of the corner of his eye, Gil saw Carlo nd Owen join Danny. They all goggled at the animatronic.

With a rumbling chirr, the robot turned its head and looked directly at Gil. The square metal-toothed mouth emitted a metallic rasp as it hinged open. "Awaiting instructions," the robot said in a flat, deep voice.

"Cool!" Danny said.

Gil turned to grin at the kid. He chuckled when he saw that Owen and Carlo were sidling away.

Gil turned back to his new robot. He leaned in and looked the robot in its radiant eyes. "I want you to break the limbs and heads off all the endoskeletons in this place and pile them up over there." He pointed toward the pile of animatronic parts by the exit door. "Easy peasy. Got it?"

The robot's internal mechanisms crackled and groaned. The robot's mouth creaked as it opened again. "Break off limbs and heads. Pile them up. Easy peasy. Got it." The robot looked directly at Gil for several seconds.

Gil shook off a sudden shiver. The robot's glow-eyed gaze was creepy. But then, the animatronic couldn't help that it didn't have a face.

The robot's joints clicked and its servos droned as it abruptly rose to its feet. Once upright, its hard metal edges reflected the stage lights behind it, making it look like it was radiating heat. To disguise an unbidden flinch, Gil quickly stood, too.

"You can start by taking inventory," Gil said to the robot.

The robot shifted its feet as if finding its balance. Something ticked into place in its midsection. Other robotic parts clacked and thrummed.

The animatronic's eyes pulsed with luminescence as it slowly and deliberately turned to scan the room. It rotated in a full circle, its gaze taking in all the robotic remains scattered throughout the space.

When the robot finished its rotation, its attention zeroed in on Gil and the other team members. The robot took a step forward, its heavy steel foot grating across the bare floor. The robot's eerie eyes locked on Gil, then moved on to Danny and then on to Owen and finally on to Carlo.

Gil's shiver returned. He glanced over at the others.

Danny's eager expression had collapsed into nervousness. He exchanged a look with Carlo, whose forehead was bunched into a worried frown. Owen wore a pinched expression that could have been annoyance . . . or fear . . . or both.

Gil had to admit he found the robot's scrutiny a little unsettling. A barely discernible wheezing sound was coming from the animatronic' s systems. Gil wasn't sure what the sound meant. Was everything functioning properly?

When the newly animated endoskeleton took a step, Gil nearly jumped out of his skin. He pretended that he'd just tripped over something, and he stepped aside as the robot strode past him.

Gil was embarrassed by his reaction, but he immediately let himself off the hook. The new endoskeleton, after all, was huge—much bigger than the five- and six-footers Gil and his

:oworkers had been dragging around for so long. It was rea-
onable for Gil's fight-or-flight response to be triggered in the
ace of that kind of power.

But there was no need for concern. The new robot was
ınder Gil's control.

Gil joined his team members as the robot, its systems grind-
ng, walked over to the nearest endoskeleton and picked it up
ıs if it was made of flimsy fabric. Effortlessly, the new cleanup
obot snapped the endoskeleton's shoulder joints. The endo-
keleton's arms came free. The robot tossed the arms aside.
They landed on the floor with a skittering clatter.

The robot did the same thing with the endoskeleton's legs,
racking the limbs from the hip joints and flinging them
oward the arms. The metal arms and legs clanked in a tangle
ıs the big robot grabbed the endoskeleton's head and popped
t off. Grasping the head between its huge metal hands, the
leanup robot rolled the skull toward the discarded limbs. As
oon as the skull stopped moving, the robot lifted the remain-
ng torso.

Stomping heavily across the black-and-white-checked
inoleum, the robot carried the torso to the pile of limbs
nd dropped it. The torso landed with a crunch and bang as
he efficient new robot turned and headed toward another
ndoskeleton.

Over the next couple minutes, the new robot made quick
work of three more endoskeletons. The robot had no problem
leconstructing the already partly broken endoskeletons and
ıdding them to the growing pile by the door.

Gil turned away from the robot. He beamed at his cowork-
rs. "See? I'm a genius!" He threw up his arms in triumph.

Danny's mom had taught him to accept and respect all
people—even the unpleasant ones. Danny didn't much like
Gil, but he pretended that he did. And now, he had to admit
hat Gil had done something pretty amazing. Even though Gil
was bragging, which was something Danny had been taught
ıot to do, ever, Gil had reason to be pleased with himself.

Danny opened his mouth to agree with Gil's self-assessment.

But he never got the words out. What happened next stole his words . . . and some of his sanity as well.

It happened so fast that it all melded together into one impossible horror that Danny's mind struggled to put into order: The robot looming. A blur of metallic motion. A squelching pop. Gil's caterwauling scream.

Danny's mind computed the events: Gil was screaming.

Because he no longer had arms.

The robot had ripped off Gil's arms.

As the robot hurled Gil's arms toward the pile of robotic parts by the pizzeria's exit door, the air left Danny's lungs, and the strength fled his legs. Danny staggered backward, his heart pounding. Not believing what he was seeing, he stared at gushing fountains of red spraying from Gil's shoulder sockets.

Beside Danny, Carlo cried out. Danny glanced toward the other two men. Owen made no sound, but his face was white. His eyes were nearly bugging out of his face.

Gil continued to scream. No, not scream. Shriek. Wail. Keen.

The sounds Gil made were unlike anything Danny had ever heard. Those sounds were accompanied by sickening cracking and crunching sounds. And even under all of that hideous racket, Danny could hear the wet slap of blood hitting the walls and the floor.

Another wrenching crunch turned Danny's thoughts into a crazed, fearful babble, especially when the crunch cut off Gil's screams completely. The crunch, which was like the twisting snap of a screw being shorn free of its housing, silenced Gil in a fraction of a second. One instant, the old pizzeria had echoed with the peals of Gil's pain. The next, the high-pitched howls were gone.

Now, all Danny could hear was his own and the others' staccato breathing. He also heard the metallic clanks and whirrs of the robot . . . which was now heading their way.

Danny, Carlo, and Owen turned as one. They started to run toward the pizzeria's only exit.

Before they took even a step, though, several construction workers poured through the open doorway, tearing into the old pizzeria. Danny and his teammates were caught between the advancing robot and the converging workers.

"What's going on down here?" one of the men called out. "We heard screams and—"

The man, a long-haired, muscle-bound bald guy Danny had seen around a few times, stopped talking when his gaze landed on the bloody carnage that used to be Gil. His eyes bulged.

"Run!" Carlo yelled.

Danny was already running. Careening through the confused and shocked men, Danny bounced off meaty arms and paunchy bellies as if he was a pinball in one of the old arcade machines.

The room was a chaos of sound and motion. Danny's senses couldn't even process it all. He only got disjointed impressions as he ran.

Danny's ears registered metallic clanks, squishy thuds, more cracks and snaps and pops, wet splashes, bellows and cries and shouts; his mind didn't even try to translate what he was hearing into actual events. He didn't want to think about it.

A stream of viscous red spewed across one of the white squares on the floor ahead of Danny. His eyes took in a galloping redheaded worker, a press of chests and faces blanched bone white . . . and a ripped-off arm—the dark skin and small oak leaf tattoo told him the arm had belonged to Carlo. When a round head tumbled across the floor in front of Danny and a grasping metal hand swiped his way, Danny darted to his left and dove between the legs of one of the panicked construction workers.

More body parts flew past. More blood sprayed.

Danny ran through a cacophony of hysteria. And everything Danny had ever learned about being polite and following the rules and respecting others was deconstructed along with the men around him. He cared about nothing but getting out of the pizzeria-turned-abattoir.

Danny dodged and dove and scrambled and flailed, and he finally reached the door. As he galloped through it, he looked back. The butchery continued. The tortured cries crescendoed. Danny blanched.

And he slammed the door.

Danny kept running. Past piles of lumber and stacks of rebar, past more converging construction workers. And then, he ran past a rumbling cement truck, its mixing drum rotating, the gray sludge of wet cement sluicing from its discharge chute.

Danny screamed at the men spreading the poured cement. "SEAL IT!"

Even shouting at the top of his lungs, Danny's words could barely be heard above the cement truck's roar and the screams that reached out from the pizzeria and curled into Danny's brain like a vine wrapping around his consciousness.

"SEAL THE DOOR!" Danny screamed louder. He pointed back toward the entry to the pizzeria.

The cement workers finally looked up. They turned and looked toward the pizzeria door.

"SEAL IT!" Danny cried out again.

And he kept running.